G g
On My Mind

Southern Promises – Book Two

KG FLETCHER

Copyright © 2018 Kelly Genelle Fletcher
All rights reserved.
ISBN-13:978-1-7320240-1-4
Printed in the United States of America.

FAIR WARNING: This book contains scenes of detailed intimacy and liberal use of profanity. It is intended for readers 18+

Georgia On My Mind
Southern Promises – Book Two

Georgia On My Mind is part of the
~Southern Promises~ collection.
Each book in the series is STANDALONE
* Georgia Clay
* Georgia On My Mind
* Georgia Pine

The characters and events in this book are fictitious. Any similarity to real persons, living or dead, places, or events is coincidental and not intended by the author.
If you purchase this book without a cover you should be aware that this book may have been stolen property and reported as "unsold and destroyed" to the publisher. In such case the author has not received any payment for this "stripped book."

Please visit my website at www.kgfletcherauthor.com

Edited by Vicky Burkholder
Cover art by Eva Talia Designs

This book, or parts thereof, may not be reproduced in any form without permission. The copying, scanning, uploading, and distribution of this book via the internet or via any other means without the permission of the publisher is illegal and punishable by law. Please purchase only authorized electronic or print editions, and do not participate in or encourage piracy of copyrighted materials. Your support of the author's rights is appreciated.

DEDICATION

For the brave and beautiful ones kicking ass every single day going after their dreams.

KG FLETCHER

CHAPTER ONE

Nodding heads and knowing smiles greeted Gia Bates as a staff member escorted her down the wide hallways of the Atlanta Country Club toward a private dining suite. Several staff and club members watched her pass with curiosity as her four-inch platform heels clicked on the marble floors and her calf-length, pleated skirt swished to the intentional, exaggerated movement of her hips. She licked her crimson lips and patted the blonde, retro-style glamour wig one last time, knowing she was seconds away from surprising an unsuspecting birthday boy. His business colleagues and friends thought it would be a hoot to hire a Marilyn Monroe strip-o-gram for the occasion, insisting on the sexiest Monroe impersonator the Atlanta entertainment company had to offer. Gia was their most popular Marilyn. She was also a pretty good Madonna, and requests regularly came in for her unforgettable "Officer Good Body" routine where she would mock-arrest an unsuspecting client, handcuffing them to a chair before blowing their minds with a memorable lap dance.

Blessed with legs that went on for days, Gia's years of dance training came in handy during specific work situations. The staff was prepared to scope out a corner of the room near the lucky recipient and to set up a small fan and sound machine by some potted plants. She heard boisterous, male laughter through a crack in the door before the clinking of glass in an apparent toast. Gia waited for a beat and took a deep breath before making her dramatic entrance into the private room.

Heads immediately turned as she posed theatrically, beveling her heeled feet and resting one hand on her hip, the other demurely holding the ivory skirt out to the side. She purposefully arched her back, pushing her chest out and accentuating her perky breasts in the plunging neckline of the halter-like bodice of the iconic Marilyn dress.

"Is there a birthday boy named Mitch Montgomery in the house?" she asked in a sultry, breathy tone.

Approximately fifteen overzealous guys were on their feet in a second, several of them slapping their friend on the back as he cautiously raised his hand.

"That would be me," he said, rolling his eyes. His buddies erupted in whoops and hollers, pushing him toward Gia. She slowly approached him with one eyebrow raised, her eyes fixated on his reddening face. Grabbing him by his loosened tie, she pulled him into the corner area and pushed him down into a vacant chair. She ran her fingers across his cheek and smiled.

"I have a little song for the birthday boy. Would you like me to sing it for you?" She batted her false eyelashes at him.

"Sure!"

More raucous racket erupted from the all-male audience who gathered as close as they could to witness the show. Gia circled the back of the chair Mitch was sitting on and placed her hands on his shoulders. When the room quieted down, she sang intimately in his ear.

"*Happy birthday to you. Happy birthday to you.*" She sang slowly, imitating the way Marilyn sang to President John F. Kennedy back in 1962. The men seemed mesmerized, all eyes on her. "*Happy birthday... Mr. Montgomery. Happy birthday to you.*"

Before anyone could say a word, Gia hit the convenient floor button of the fan and straddled it, making the skirt of her costume lift and billow, replicating the famous scene in the 1955 Marilyn Monroe movie, *The Seven Year Itch.*

"Oh!" she squealed, leaning forward and shaking her breasts for everyone. The entire room went crazy. With another push of a button, the jazzy instrumental song, *The Stripper*, blared out of a small Bose speaker. The famous trombone slides set up the next part of the show—the striptease.

Reaching behind her neck, Gia unclasped the halter of her cocktail dress and let it fall seductively forward, exposing her gorgeous lingerie beneath. Mitch threw his head back and laughed before she turned around and sat on his lap.

"Would you mind unzipping me, handsome?" she teased, looking over her shoulder at him.

"Not at all!" He enthusiastically pulled the zipper down as his friends shouted, lifting their glasses in the air.

Shimmying out of her dress, she held Mitch's hand while stepping over the pile of fabric that now lay on the floor. Her encrusted rhinestone bodice hugged her curves, and her fishnet stockings accentuated her long, lean legs. She danced and gyrated all around Mitch, pulling him by the tie and ruffling his hair, aware of the cat-calls and whistles. A couple of his friends handed him wads of cash that he happily stuffed into her cleavage and the bottom of her bodice when she would purposefully bend over in front of him. The entire PG-13 tease lasted less than five minutes, ending with Gia still covered in more clothing than when she was at the beach. The sophisticated lingerie, stockings, and shoes were an illusion of sorts. It was the way she used her body, especially her long legs, teasing her male audience, that produced the sensual fantasy.

When the song ended, she pulled Mitch up from the chair and grabbed him by the face, forcefully planting red lip stamps on both his cheeks. She held his hand and swung it ceremoniously in the air before bending forward in a final bow to the roar of applause.

As if on cue, the staff of the country club rolled in a huge sheet-cake lit with candles, and the men erupted in another boisterous rendition of the happy birthday song, raising glasses and beer bottles into the air. Gia quickly pulled the cash out of her cleavage and buttocks before slipping back into her show dress. By the time Mitch had made a wish and blown out the candles, she was poised and ready to take photos with the crowd of men who had ogled her just minutes before.

Waiters and waitresses passed out generous slices of cake and came around with trays of shots, the men eagerly grabbing the tiny glasses. Mitch's face flushed as he approached her and handed her one.

"Here, Marilyn. You deserve it."

She batted her lashes at him, offering a shy smile. "Why, thank you, Mitch. You're a doll." They clinked glasses and downed the shots in one gulp. The expensive bourbon was delicious on her tongue, and she welcomed the warmth and courage it gave her to continue in the unusual job setting.

As the men continued to drink and eat cake, Gia posed over the fan while a few of the guys took the opportunity to stand next to her for a photo op. An hour after she arrived, the group dispersed onto the veranda for authentic Cuban cigars. She gave Mitch one last hug and wished him well. The staff manager helped gather her props and walk her back through the club toward the lobby. He stopped by the intricate iron double front doors and pulled a white envelope out of his suit jacket.

"You did a great job tonight. The client wanted you to have this and to thank you for using your…assets in the birthday surprise."

"Oh, great!" She took the envelope from his hands, surprised when his index finger purposefully brushed hers.

Eyeing him cautiously, she watched as he looked around quickly before boldly taking a step forward and speaking with a low voice near her ear. "You got any plans tonight? I've heard some of you gals from the entertainment company like to party afterward." His breath was disgusting as he spoke. Usually, it was a drunk party guest who would cross the line. That it happened to be the staff manager of the reputable club tonight miffed her.

"Uh, yes. Unfortunately, I do have plans. Thanks for everything!" Quickly, she turned on her heels and started for the door. The man grabbed her by the arm, causing her to swing her head around and scowl at him in protest. "Stop it!" His clammy fingers dug into her flesh, and she knew there'd be a bruise on that part of her arm in the morning because her porcelain skin bruised easily and his grip was strong enough to leave a mark. "What are you doing?"

Keeping a firm grip on her arm, he leaned in and whispered gruffly, "Come on. I could show you a really good time. I got the keys to this place. And I've got cash for you. We could have our own party…"

"*Asshole*!" she shouted, bringing her knee to his groin and sending him to the floor.

"Ah, fuck!" he squeaked, grabbing his crotch. He fell to his knees and rocked back and forth on the expensive marble in obvious pain.

"Is there a problem, miss?"

Gia was panting, adrenaline flooding her system as she watched a tall, dark and handsome man approach. Dressed in an expensive suit with his red tie loosened around his neck, she couldn't help but stare at him with wide eyes. Too stunned to speak, she gestured to the asshole on the ground.

A repulsed look crossed his masculine features as he looked at the man writhing on the floor before he turned his attention back to her, concern clouding his face. "Are you all right?" His eyes were big and brown; his chiseled face sharp in the chandelier light.

"I'm...I'm fine. This idiot made a pass at me." She stood a bit taller and finally exhaled. "I kicked him in the nuts."

The handsome man chuckled as his eyes raked her up and down. "I didn't know Ms. Monroe was such a bad-ass."

Gia bit her tongue to keep from smiling.

"As for you, mister. I'm going to need to talk to your supervisor." He grabbed the manager roughly by the arm and pulled him to his feet.

"I *am* the fucking supervisor," he gasped, obviously still in pain from the way he was doubled over.

By this time, several curious staff members had wandered into the lobby to see what the fuss was all about. Gia watched as her rescuer spoke with a couple of them who immediately called for backup. The guy she had kneed had managerial status in the food service department, but he was not ultimately in charge. When the Director of Club Services arrived, another employee escorted the staff manager to an office nearby, out of the public eye and gripping his precious groin the entire time. Gia assured the director she didn't want to call the police or press charges. She just wanted to get to her car safely and go home.

As the people in the lobby dispersed, Gia held her hand out to the man who had stepped in on her behalf. "Thank you for being at the right place at the right time."

His broad smile revealed perfect, white teeth. He gently took Gia's hand and shook it. "My pleasure, Marilyn Monroe." His eyes sparkled.

"I'm not really Marilyn." She said as she twitched her skirt from side to side.

"You're not?" His expression drooped with humorous disappointment. "I could have sworn you were the real thing."

Shaking her head, she giggled. "You're funny. And I'm Gia."

"Gia…"

The sound of her name coming out of his beautiful mouth caused her breath to hitch.

"I'm Hart."

"Heart?" She couldn't have heard him correctly. "Like a beating heart?"

He chuckled. "No. Hart. Short for Hartford. It's a pleasure to meet you, Gia."

There it was again—the exhale of her name on his lips. It was intimate and sexy as hell, as if they were lying next to each other in bed and he was whispering sweet nothings in her ear. She stared into his brown eyes, lost in the moment.

"Can I walk you to your car?" He was looking back at her with an amusing expression.

She shook her head, jolting her brain back to reality. "Sure. I mean, yes. That would be nice."

GEORGIA ON MY MIND

CHAPTER TWO

Hartford Parker helped Gia navigate the stairs in her high heels by holding her sturdily by the elbow. The early spring night air was chilly, and he felt her shiver beneath his touch. He hadn't been this close to a woman in months and couldn't help but admire the way her hips swayed as she walked ahead of him across the black asphalt. The streetlights illuminated the parking lot, the moonlight blotted by the cloudy sky.

He had been looking forward to Mitch's birthday celebration at the club, especially knowing there were a couple guys from some prestigious brokerage firms attending. What better way to bend a colleague's ear and do a little networking than after a couple rounds of drinks? It had been eight months since Hart was let go from his lucrative job in DC. He had moved back to Atlanta and still hadn't landed, living off his severance and house-sitting for his sister. Losing his job at one of the top firms in the country after a scandalous encounter with a client's daughter at a party was probably the worst thing he had ever endured. Luckily for him, he had been given a generous severance package—a testament to the millions of dollars he had procured for the company over the five years he worked for them. Unfortunately, his indiscretion was the talk of the town for several embarrassing months, causing him to lie low until he felt it was time to start putting his career back together. To his disappointment, the two guys he had his eye on at the party were more interested in getting shit-faced than talking business. At least he got their cards and a handshake promise to meet for lunch in the near future. He was anxious to turn the page and finally put the past behind him. The climax of the evening was helping a beautiful damsel in distress—well, distress was a stretch because she could obviously hold her own.

"This is me," Gia said, bringing him out of his thoughts. She was standing next to a well-worn sedan, a shade lighter than her blue eyes. "I got it from here."

"Cool." Hart shifted uncomfortably in the night air, not sure how to ask for her phone number after the fiasco in the club. In addition to lying low from his business colleagues, he had also sworn off women as a self-induced punishment. But there was something about Gia that drew him in, and he wanted to get to know her. Perhaps it was time to free himself from his jail.

When she first entered the private dining room in her Marilyn Monroe get-up, he had to admit, he felt sorry for her. He never understood why a beautiful girl would stoop to dancing or strip for money. After seeing her act and how professional she was, he was curious and had questions. There was nothing sleazy or raunchy about Gia. She was a character playing a part and did a damn good job! Her beautiful legs went on for days, and her delicious curves were perfection. Her eyes—her eyes were another story. He had never seen such intense eyes that color blue before. There was a story behind those eyes, and he was determined to learn more.

"You done for the night or are you heading home?"

She threw her props into the back seat of the vehicle and turned to him, rubbing her hands up and down her bare arms. "This was my only gig tonight, thank God. I have to be up early for a class in the morning," she replied, matter-of-factly.

"Oh?" he replied, surprised. "You're a student?" He silently chastised himself for his stereotypical view of her Marilyn get-up, relieved she was probably only doing this for extra money to put herself through school.

She paused, her perfect brow raised slightly. "No. I'm the teacher."

His eyes widened in response, rendering him speechless.

She laughed at his reaction. "I teach ballet."

"Of course, you do. I would have totally pegged you as a dancer by the way you so elegantly walk and move." Heat rose on the back of his neck. What was she doing to him? In order to change the subject, Hart boldly reached up to her wig and fingered the platinum tresses. "I'm curious. What is your real hair color?"

Gia smiled, her blue eyes darker under the street lights. "Wouldn't you like to know?" she teased.

He laughed and pushed his hands deep into his pants pockets, smitten by the banter between him and Gia. "Can I buy you a cup of coffee? There are a couple of places not far from here and the night is still young." He noticed her hesitation. "I promise, I won't make a pass at you."

"Don't you have a party to get back to? What will Mitch Montgomery think?"

"Mitch will be fine. I'll see him next week on the golf course." He boldly took off his suit jacket and started to hang it over her shoulders. Gia pulled back.

"You're cold," he said softly. "My jacket is warm."

She hesitated a second more before nodding and allowing him to finish, her creamy shoulders snuggling into the clothing.

"One cup of coffee. That's all I'm asking. You can follow me in your own car."

"You're a real Southern gentleman, aren't you Hart?"

Her smile was genuine, as if touched by his gesture.

"My mother and father raised me right," he joked. If she only knew his whole scandalous story, she might perceive his comment as a bold-faced lie. Hart opened the car door and watched her ease into the front seat. "Now if you'll just follow me, I promise there will be more chivalry to come." He pressed his fist to his chest and leaned over dramatically in a sweeping bow, making her laugh.

Gia relented. "Okay. One cup of coffee."

"Okay?"

She nodded. "Yes. Don't drive too fast."

"I'll go nice and slow," he reassured her. He shut Gia's door and trotted to his Mercedes a few spaces away, pleased she had accepted his offer. When he pulled out, he waited till she was right behind him before leaving the club premises.

They wove their way through the upper-class neighborhood to the main streets of the city, only having to stop at two red lights. Hart was about to turn into the nearest Starbucks he prayed might still be open, but when he saw the infamous red light ahead of him, he let out a whoop inside his car. "Yes!"

They parked side by side at the Krispy Kreme donut shop, the red "hot now" light blazing in all its glory. When he came around to open the car door for Gia, he was stunned when she climbed out. She had taken the blonde Marilyn wig off, her jet-black hair stopping him in his tracks. The striking chin-length bob with short bangs accentuated her vivid blue eyes, and with the white dress, fishnets, and red lipstick, she looked like she had just stepped out of a time machine from the 1920s.

"Black," she said, pointing to her head, her eyes wide as if anticipating his reaction.

"Gorgeous," he replied in a whisper, drinking in her striking image. He stood there with his mouth hanging open, staring. Gia was *nothing* like any of the girls he had ever accompanied. She was mysterious and jaw-droppingly

12

stunning in a unique way.

"Are we going in?" she asked, holding his jacket taut around her shoulders.

Hart closed his mouth quickly. "Yes! Shall we?" He offered his bent elbow, which she took, and they headed toward the free-standing building. "We're so in luck. The 'hot now' light is on!"

"What's the 'hot now' light?"

He stopped near the curb. "Are you kidding me? You don't know about the 'hot now' light?"

"Afraid not."

He scratched his head and grinned. Placing his hand on her shoulder, he turned her around and pointed at the circular neon light in the window. "When the red 'hot now' light is on, it means the donuts just came out of the oven. If you've never experienced a hot, glazed Krispy Kreme donut fresh out of the oven, you're in for the biggest treat of your life!"

She laughed out loud. "If you say so!"

Several minutes later, they sat across from each other in a corner booth, holding cups of hot coffee and eyeing a box full of a half-dozen donuts still steaming from the oven. Hart was astonished at how striking Gia was in the fluorescent lighting of the place. Her flawless skin was luminescent and her eyes… god, he could get lost in those eyes. Several patrons did double-takes, noticing her. She looked so different from the average Atlanta woman. If he hadn't met her already and were a stranger walking in, he would assume she was a celebrity of some kind. She stuck out like a sore thumb still wearing her white dress, fishnets, and heels. She was like an exotic white orchid surrounded by the hardscape of the city.

He lifted two donuts out of the box and handed her one. "On the count of three, I want you to take a big bite and savor it. Roll it all around in your mouth and tell me what you think."

She nodded, and their eyes locked in on each other.

"One, two, three." As they bit into their donuts at the same time, Hart couldn't help himself and moaned when the hot glaze hit his tongue. He closed his eyes and chewed slowly, savoring the distinct flavor of his favorite childhood treat. When he opened his eyes, Gia's reaction thrilled him. She looked like she was suppressing a smile as she chewed, a film of glaze stuck to her upper lip. She nodded eagerly.

"Wow! How did I not know about this?" she said with her mouth full.

"I know. It's a confectionary wonder. My grandparents used to take my sister and me every Sunday morning before church. The taste reminds me of my youth." He gazed at her and homed in on the filmy layer of glaze stuck to her lip. Brazenly, he reached across the table and wiped it off with the pad of his thumb. Her chest rose in a deep breath as if surprised by his bold move. She took a paper napkin out of the dispenser and wiped it across her mouth, staining the paper with red lipstick.

"Thanks," she said quietly, a pinkish hue crossing her pale cheeks.

He stuck his thumb in his mouth and licked off the glaze, eyeing her purposefully. Had he gone too far? "You're welcome."

The subtle blush on her pale skin and the demure smile she tried to hide were encouraging as they continued to eat their donuts and sip coffee. Hart leaned back in the booth, propping both arms up on the seat. "So, are you from around here?"

Gia smiled shyly and set her cup down before licking her lips. "I've been here for a while."

"Okay." He shifted, bringing his arms forward and wrapping them around his cup. "How long have you been performing as Marilyn?" Waiting with bated breath, he produced his best smoldering gaze.

She confidently tipped her chin up, raising a perfect eyebrow. It was a sultry mannerism from his own playbook, one he thoroughly enjoyed being on the receiving end of. "I've been performing as Marilyn for almost a year now."

Hart nodded. "Cool. I guess the money is good, huh?" Curiosity was killing him. He wanted to know why she performed as Marilyn and what motivated her to dance so seductively in a room full of guys. Money had to be the answer.

"The money is decent. It helps supplement the rising costs of everything," Gia replied, fingering the top of her cup with a vibrant red fingernail. "What about you? What do you do to have such a nice car?"

Touché, he thought. Tit for tat. She was not like any other girl he had ever been with. He was going to have to work hard if he wanted to get to know her.

"I'm a real estate broker. Made good bank in DC for the past five years. I'm back in Atlanta now, looking for a fresh start."

She eyed him dubiously, and he thought she was about to ask for more details. Instead, she reached into the box and pulled out another donut. "I know all about fresh starts." Staring directly at him, she deliberately took a big bite, making him chuckle nervously.

Hartford Parker was a playboy able to reel in the ladies without much effort. Now, he was barely treading water, nervous and almost giddy around Gia. Who was this girl?

GEORGIA ON MY MIND

CHAPTER THREE

All ten channels on Gia's ancient television were broadcasting nothing but infomercials, the light from the perky images of commentators bouncing off the dark walls of her tiny, makeshift living space at the back end of her dance studio. She had given up her apartment several months ago, the increase in rent too much to handle in addition to the rising lease payments and staff salaries of her small business. After rolling up her sleeves, she cleaned out an oversized storage closet and set up her new home. She added an expensive new lock only she had the key to, hoping her property manager and staff would never find out. The couch barely fit, taking up one whole wall, and there was just enough room for a bookshelf and table. Everything else she owned she stored in boxes stacked up against the wall in the small kitchenette she and her remaining two dance instructors used to take breaks between classes. Dancing had always been her passion, ever since she was a young girl. To be able to parlay her expertise into a business was a lot harder than she ever expected. The years of many classes and auditions were nothing compared to the stress of running her own company. Glancing over her shoulder, she sighed and reminded herself that the bright side of living at her work was dancing anytime, day or night, in the large student space with entire walls of mirrors.

After clicking off the TV, she snuggled into the threadbare sofa she also used as her bed, strategically covered in brightly colored sheets and pillows. She dreaded the long, endless nights at the end of the day, tossing and turning while her mind replayed her financial woes in her wakefulness. At least her mind was wandering to thoughts of Hartford Parker, the tall, dark, and handsome donut-eating gentleman who had somehow convinced her to give him her number. It was nice having something different to think about for a change. Her eyes adjusted to the dark room as she lay back on a pillow and lazily went over the night in her mind.

He had been so sweet, stepping in at just the right moment at the country club before the low-life manager with bad breath groped her inappropriately. When Hart put his suit jacket around her cold, bare shoulders after escorting her to her car, she knew she'd end up giving him her number at some point in the evening—he just had to ask for it, which, of course, he did. In a long line of suitors, he ranked first among those who interested her. Standing in the empty parking lot at the Krispy Kreme with a sugar-high like no other, she recalled Hart boldly leaning in and kissing her on the mouth, his warm lips lingering with a sweetness she hadn't experienced in a very long time. He wanted to see her again—and as soon as possible. She wanted to see him too, their mutual chemistry dismissing his lofty promise not to make a pass. Their flirtatious evening paved the way for small permissions and innocent gestures. But was she ready to invite a total stranger into her stressful world?

Immediately, her eyes darted to the shadowed pile of bills on the table and her thoughts reverted to her usual angst. It had been two long months since she had taken a paycheck from her failing dance studio. She had agreed to more gigs with the entertainment company to help cover some of her expenses, especially her staff salaries, her second job bringing in the most money. Unfortunately, the owner of the company never paid on time, and it was usually up to her to track him down to get a check. In addition to his entertainment business, the owner of the entertainment company, Franko Bartelli, also owned a thriving strip club off Highway 141 near the perimeter of the city. Every time she saw him, he was always trying to convince her to join his lineup of girls at the club. Tempted on her worst days because she knew the money would be outrageous, deep down she could never fathom stooping to that level. She took pride in her studio, which offered a variety of classes ranging from basic ballet and contemporary dance to jazz and tap. She also taught a couple of adult classes on Wednesday evenings to those daring couples wanting to learn the waltz or swing dance. She knew without-a-doubt that none of her students had a clue regarding her "extra" work as a Madonna or Marilyn impersonator. If any of the suburban moms of her youngest students got wind of what she did on the side, she'd lose her business for sure. Rolling her eyes, she knew she'd have to make an appearance at the strip club where the entertainment company main office was located and beg Franko for a check that was rightfully hers.

Staring up at the white popcorn ceiling barely illuminated in the dark by her alarm clock, Gia sighed and thought about her little piece of heaven. The location of her studio in an ancient strip mall was off the beaten path. Because it was so old and left to her in her late Aunt Caroline's will, she got a steal on the lease agreement, her payment including utilities much to her excitement. It didn't take long for her to realize the surrounding area was slowly deteriorating and people were relocating to the more popular areas of town. Most of the retailers near her had gone out of business, and she was one of only six businesses left in the crumbling real estate, doing the best she could to stay afloat.

It was four in the morning when sleep started to tug on her heavy eyelids. Gia blinked slowly and wondered if she had just hit pay dirt meeting Hart that night. He had to be wealthy if he belonged to the country club. And he drove a Mercedes. She shook her head quickly, shame spreading through her entire being. She was not a gold-digger, and no matter how tempting, she would never deliberately date a man because he had cash. Convinced that money was the root of all evil, she felt that people stooped to sordid levels to acquire it. Her late mother was proof of that. As the clock struck five a.m., Gia rolled onto her side, her mind finally shutting down.

***

Hart tried to hold his cell phone to his ear, balancing it between his head and shoulder as he tied his running shoes. His sister, Katie, was going on and on about her latest stop in Chicago to let him know another postcard was on the way. He loved his only sister and was extremely happy for her new life with Grammy-award-winning country artist, "Georgia" Clay Watkins. The two were inseparable since she joined him on tour this past Christmas, Clay encouraging her to accompany him on a once-in-a-lifetime adventure on the road. Katie threw caution to the wind and gave up her corporate insurance job and was now hobnobbing with a famous country touring artist. Hart knew it was only a matter of time before the two would get hitched, their love for each other something he hoped for in his own life someday.

"Well, I'll be sure to look for it in the mail," he said, referring to the postcard and grinning from ear to ear. "And yes, your ferns are doing well. I'm only watering them once a week as you said."

When his shoes were tied, he sat up and palmed the phone in his hand. "I love you too, baby girl. Give Clay my best."

The siblings said their goodbyes before he clicked the

off button. He sighed and looked around his sister's condo. She had graciously offered him the job of house-sitting while she was on the road for the next several months and he was in transition. A side perk of house-sitting was not having to pay a sky-high lease every month for his own place. Add to that a great location in Northeast Atlanta, and he was set for the time being.

He shrugged on an old Atlanta Falcons sweatshirt and headed out the door into the crisp, spring morning. Once he was out of the gated community, he started to jog. Atlanta commuters were already lined up on the four-lane streets, trying to get to work in the early morning. He couldn't help but feel lucky not to be stuck in his car in brutal traffic, able to work out and do whatever he damned well pleased. For the moment, anyway.

Hart jogged around the corner and darted into a small park he had stumbled upon a few weeks earlier. It was always deserted this time of day, the suburban moms still stuck in carpool lines dropping off older siblings before bringing their toddlers out for some fresh air. As his feet padded along the sidewalk among the tall Georgia pines and budding azalea bushes about to pop with bursts of color, his mind wandered to Gia. He was contemplating texting her and asking her to lunch, or dinner. Maybe drinks would be more to her liking, unless she had a gig. A smile spread across his face as he thought about her. He hoped that whatever it was he proposed, she would say "yes." He wanted to take his time and get to know her. There was something intriguing behind her vivid eyes; the blue reminding him of an unforgettable vacation to Italy when he experienced the famous waters of the blue grotto for the first time. He wanted to dive in, ready to take on a challenge, his pace quickening, his heart pumping his fiery blood through his pulsing veins.

After jogging several miles, pushing his body harder than ever, he stopped to catch his breath at the crosswalk that would take him home. As he waited for the light to change, his phone vibrated in his shorts. Panting, he squinted in the morning light, not recognizing the number. He inhaled deeply before answering.

"This is Hartford Parker." A huge garbage truck squealed by, making him stick his index finger into his free ear. "Hello? Can you hear me?"

"Hey, Hart. It's Gia. The girl from last night."

Hart couldn't help himself and smiled wide. "Gia? Hey! How are you?" For her to call him the morning after their first meeting was a good sign. It meant she was interested.

"I'm fine, thanks. Did I catch you at a bad time?"

As the garbage truck disappeared over a hill, he took his finger out of his ear and ran his hand through his sweaty hair. "No. No, I'm just finishing up my morning jog in the local park. Sorry about the loud traffic."

She giggled on the other end. "That's okay."

The two didn't say anything for a beat while Hart paced. "I'd like to see you again, Gia. Is that possible?"

"Yes. That's why I'm calling. I still have your suit jacket and wanted to get it back to you."

"Oh. Yes, that's right." His face fell with disappointment as he realized she was just calling to make arrangements to get his jacket back to him. He sat on the park bench across from the Marta bus stop and used his sleeve to wipe the sweat profusely running down his face.

"I'd also like to take you to lunch sometime, as a 'thank you' for last night. You went above and beyond the call of chivalry by introducing me to those donuts."

He couldn't help but laugh out loud, his spirits lifting immediately. "I'd love to join you for lunch, Gia. As a matter-of-fact, I'm free today. Can you meet me today?" He hoped he wasn't pushing it, but his father always told him to strike when the iron was hot. And she was hot!

"Sure. I can make that happen. I'll text you the address of a place I think you'll like and you can meet me there."

"Sounds like a plan." Relief washed over him, knowing he was going to see the mysterious woman again. "I'll be there at noon."

"Perfect. I'll see you soon, Hart."

"See ya, Gia." He waited until she hung up first and couldn't help but whoop out loud and fist-bump the air. When he looked back at his phone, he realized he finally had something to look forward to. So much so, he planned on being fashionably early.

GEORGIA ON MY MIND

CHAPTER FOUR

Hart parked his car near the entrance of the free-standing diner, making sure to lock it, his Mercedes sticking out like a shiny new toy in a dumpster. The funny thing was, he knew this area well. His years as a young, impressionable boy riding along with his father, accompanying him on real estate deals quickly came to mind. That was back in the days of a stiff drink and a handshake which was as good as any signed legal document today. He couldn't help but smile, reminiscing about an innocent time in his life, looking up to the one man who had always been and always would be larger than life to him. He also couldn't help but assess the area, just as his father would have. The free-standing building was smack dab in the middle of the parking lot with a long row of stores in an aging strip mall behind it. It was an eclectic mix of shops situated in the run-down area. The old, outdated signage and several vacant businesses made him sad in a way. Back in the day, Hart remembered the surrounding community as vibrant, the streets and shops full of life. Now, the area looked like it was on its last leg, the deteriorating structures, and vacant homes nearby more of an eyesore. Because of the recent recession, Hart wondered if some of the landlords became too cash-strapped to spend money on the upkeep. Following in the footsteps of his father as a once-successful real estate broker, Hart automatically went through a checklist of what would bring the area back to life: some painting and parking restriping, façade renovations, and creative marketing first and foremost. Perhaps renegotiating tax incentives with the local government would bring some new life into the area? He chuckled, realizing he missed being in the business world. It was time to make an effort and get back in the game. His thoughts were quickly dashed again to present day. Looking around at the crumbling, unappealing real estate, he couldn't help but think about his own career that was in the toilet. With everything Hart had been through in the last six months, it was a wonder his father hadn't disowned him outright, his disapproving glares and comments almost too much to bear. It would take Mr. Parker, Sr. a very long time to get over Hart's indiscretions and the embarrassment he had caused the family. That, and the fact Hart was officially unemployed and living with his sister.

As he pulled the diner door open, the mouth-watering aroma of home-cooking hit him, and he inhaled deeply. His thoughts shifted to the woman waiting inside. Standing tall on the ancient linoleum-covered floor in the small foyer, Hart looked around the interior of the place, his stomach grumbling with hunger—and butterflies. It was odd feeling anxious. He was usually so calm, cool, and collected around the ladies. His pulse quickened as he searched the diner, but there was no sign of Gia. He decided to go ahead and get the corner booth by a large window, anticipating his reunion with her. A curvy African-American woman with a definite swing in her step brought him a glass of water, her Southern drawl comforting.

"Just you today or are you waitin' for others?" she asked.

Hart smiled looking up at her. "I'm waiting for someone. She should be here any…" He was interrupted when the waitress suddenly laughed out loud, holding her arms out. To his surprise, Gia walked straight into her embrace and they bear-hugged.

"It's so good to see you, sweet girl! It's been too long." Gia winked at him with her chin on the waitress's shoulder before pulling back and shaking her head as she continued to clasp hands with the waitress. "I'm so glad you're back, Angel. You were sorely missed around this place. Are you getting your strength back? You look *good*!"

"Gettin' better every day." Angel grinned revealing a gap between her teeth. Her eyes darted back to Hart, and she inhaled quickly. "I'm so sorry, sir. I was askin' if you were waitin' on anyone or if you were flyin' solo?"

Gia slowly eased herself into the seat across from him with a look of chagrin. "I'm joining him, Angel. This is my new friend, Hart."

Angel's eyes widened in surprise, and she placed her hand on her hip. "Oh! Well, I'll be right back with another glass of water and some menus."

"Thanks, Angel."

Once she was out of earshot, Gia leaned back against the booth and looked right at him. He was at a loss for words and had to slowly inhale as he took in her undeniable beauty. Her face was scrubbed clean of the show makeup she'd been wearing the night before, her rosebud lips and porcelain skin breathtaking. Her raven hair was tucked over one ear, the other side falling stick straight to her jawline. The short, black bangs were a stark contrast against the paleness of her skin, and the blueness of her eyes was warmer than before, as if she were happy or well-rested. He wanted to get lost in those eyes and drink in the heavenly aroma that surrounded her. It would be so easy to reach his hand across the table and caress her soft cheek.

A perfectly arched eyebrow jolted him out of his

daydream as she stared back at him. "You look nice today, Mr. Parker."

He cleared his throat and couldn't help but smirk. "You look good too, Ms. Bates." His voice was low and rumbled.

She blushed, biting her dewy lip. "Thanks. And thanks for meeting me for lunch. I believe this belongs to you." She passed his suit jacket across the table. They smiled awkwardly at each other, Hart taking the clothing from her hands.

Angel arrived back at their booth and placed a glass of water in front of Gia before handing them menus. "So, we have a meat and three special today. Just three-ninety-nine, your choice of fried chicken, pork chops or meatloaf. Comes with three sides and a biscuit or cornbread. If you want something lighter, like Ms. Bates usually orders, I got some real good egg salad or pimento cheese."

"The egg salad is the bomb," Gia offered, handing the menu back to Angel.

"Then, I'll have the same thing." Hart looked up at the waitress who was pursing her lips with delight and handed back the menu.

"Well, now. That was easy." She started to jot down their order on a small pad. "Two egg salad sandwiches on toasted wheat. Comes with homemade kettle chips or fruit, but I'll bring out both so you can share. Anything other than water to drink? How about some sweet tea? It's the best."

"Sure," Hart replied.

"I'm good with water," Gia added, ripping the paper off a plastic straw.

Hart noticed Angel bump Gia's shoulder with her fist in a friendly manner as she walked away.

"What was wrong with your friend?" he asked curiously, finally settling down.

Gia puckered her lips around the straw pulling in a gulp of water before responding. "She was in a wreck on

Interstate 285. It almost killed her."

"God, that's terrible. She does look good after something like that."

"Yeah. It's nice to have her back."

Angel dropped off Hart's sweet tea.

"So, do you live around here?" He wanted to get to know Gia Bates. She was kind and thoughtful, but there was something else behind her shimmery, blue gaze he was determined to get to the bottom of.

"You could say that. I own a business in the strip mall across the parking lot."

"*Really?*" Hart was surprised. Not only did she perform as Marilyn Monroe and teach ballet, but she owned a business in this neighborhood. There was a story behind that. "What kind of business?"

"It's a dance studio. It's where I teach ballet."

Hart had assumed she was a hired teacher at a dance studio, not the owner of the business. He leaned forward, resting his elbows on the Formica tabletop, and listened intently as Gia told him all about her profession. He didn't even notice the restaurant fill up with the lunchtime crowd or the second refill of sweet tea Angel brought to him, mesmerized and impressed by Gia's history as a classically trained ballerina in her youth. Her joy and love of dancing were evident in the way her eyes sparkled when she talked about it. It was as if a fire hydrant had opened, pouring out countless stories she shared of her years as a dancer. He was confused when she told him her ultimate dream as a teen had been to become an iconic Radio City Rockette.

"Why a Rockette?" he asked. "Why not the lead ballerina in *Swan Lake* or something?"

Gia giggled. "I don't know. I love ballet, but I like other styles of dance just as much. I was always fascinated watching the Rockettes during the Macy's Thanksgiving Day parade on television when I was growing up. There was just something so magical and cool about their camaraderie and precision. They're like a family, you know? The Radio City Rockettes are an institution dating back to the 1930s. They're part of history and there's nothing else like them in any other job in show business. I just had to try."

"Had you ever even been to the Big Apple before?" Hart asked with his mouth full of the most delicious egg salad.

"No," she replied, wiping her face with a paper napkin. "It was god awful. I had never been anywhere other than Georgia in my entire life and had no idea what I was doing. It's another level in that city—the dance business is very cut-throat, and the audition process is grueling. I didn't last very long."

"But did you at least try out for the Rockettes?" His brow furrowed, trying to imagine Gia in New York City.

"No, I didn't. I wasn't ready. I did get to see *The Radio City Christmas Spectacular* Starring the Rockettes though. It was a highlight of my time there. I guess you could say I gained some confidence going through all those auditions and taking classes. When I got back to Atlanta, I auditioned for the TV show, *So You Think You Can Dance*. Made it into the top twenty."

His heart surged with pride, and he stopped eating. "That's amazing!"

Gia blushed, averting her eyes and shaking her head. "It was pretty surreal. After New York and my time on TV, I thought I might go back to New York or try LA and go further with dance, you know, as a career. But then my aunt got sick, and I took care of her and maintained the studio in her last months. When she died, she left the studio to me in her will. I pretty much gave up on my professional dance dream." Her head was cocked to the side as she looked at him thoughtfully. "You want to see it?"

"See what?" he answered, nerves settling into his gut, making the delicious egg salad less appetizing.

"My studio?" He watched her pull money out of a

small purse and set it on the table.

"Please, Gia. Let me pay," he pleaded. She had caught him off guard, his chivalry slipping.

"No, Hart. I told you, this is my way of saying, 'thank you' for last night."

As they stood and gathered their things, he was aware of how independent she was. It was refreshing and daunting at the same time. He realized at that moment, she never really needed his help to begin with.

GEORGIA ON MY MIND

CHAPTER FIVE

They walked silently in-between several cars across the parking lot that had seen better days. Gia almost didn't share with Hart about her time in New York and her stint on the TV dance show, his apparent shock evident in his handsome face and quiet demeanor. She wasn't trying to show off or impress him. He was just very easy to talk to. She had asked him to meet at her favorite diner conveniently located near her business, not only to treat him to a thank-you lunch but to get his opinion on her current real estate. Even though they hadn't spent much time together, she caught on quickly that he had been some sort of big-shot as a real estate broker at one time and hoped he might be able to give her some good advice.

"This is it," she said proudly, pointing up to the red and white cursive Dance Atlanta logo on the awning. She still couldn't get over the fact that this little piece of brick and mortar belonged to her. The outside was deceiving, the inside well-cared for and immaculately clean. She turned the key to the door and flicked on a bank of lights.

The main room was a large, open space with wall-to-wall mirrors. A worn ballet barre was on one side, and a small, upright piano sat in the corner near a tall bookshelf loaded with an old sound-system and several trophies.

Hart whistled through his teeth. "This is huge, Gia. I would have never known this place existed behind the brick wall out front. How long have you been here?"

Gia set her purse down on top of the piano. "Most of my life." She couldn't help but smile, a surge of warm love penetrating her being. Her Aunt Caroline had started the business back in the 1980s when leg-warmers and headbands were all the rage. When Gia was born a decade later, she was practically raised in the studio, which became her sanctuary during her teens after her mother died. Her aunt became her guardian in those years, mentoring her passion for dance and celebrating the milestones she achieved along the way. It had been two years since her Aunt's passing; the business left to Gia in the will. She was determined to keep it afloat, but with the recent economic downturn, she was struggling.

Hart stood in the middle of the room. He clutched his suit jacket with one hand, the other on his hip, and looked around. "How many square feet do you have?" Gia thought he looked cute in his collared shirt and khakis. He was a real preppy Southern boy looking out of place in the unadorned space.

"Almost fifteen-hundred. I have a small bathroom and kitchenette in the back as well as some storage and an office. We make it work."

Hart turned his gaze toward her and approached. She couldn't help but admire his chiseled jawline and dark, smoky eyes. Even casually dressed, he was an incredibly handsome man. "Who's 'we'?"

Gia nodded. "My staff. Or what's left of them." She watched his brow furrow.

"What do you mean?"

She sighed and rested her arm on the piano. "You could probably tell that this area didn't fare too well during the recession."

His eyebrows raised as if in agreement. "Yes. I gathered

that when I arrived in the parking lot." He approached the opposite end of the piano, placing his jacket on top and mirrored her stance, resting his arm on the sturdy wood. "You said you've been here most of your life. Did you grow up in the surrounding neighborhood?"

Gia nodded. "Yes. I used to ride my bike here back in the day. This place belonged to my Aunt Caroline, and when I was old enough, I was one of her instructors, teaching basic ballet and tap to the little ones. She left it to me when she died a couple years ago." Her eyes misted. "I was the only one in the family that ever had her passion for dance. I was the logical choice, I guess." She didn't want to go into her family history and left it at that.

"Wow. And you've kept it going all this time? That's quite a feat, Gia."

Her cheeks heated as she looked at him, the chemistry between them palpable. "It hasn't been easy, that's for sure. I only have two teachers left, and they work part-time. I'm pretty much the head honcho around here."

"How do you manage your other work? You know, as Marilyn." His face showed genuine concern.

"My Marilyn gigs help with the rising costs of the studio. I wish I could just be a dance instructor and call it a day, but…" She shrugged.

"But you're a responsible adult with her own business. It's impressive, Gia. You're impressive."

She forced air out of her nose, suppressing a nervous chuckle and looked at the floor. She didn't realize he had crossed the space between them until his fingertips cupped her chin and she raised her head, looking at him with wide eyes, holding her breath.

"You impress me," he reiterated in a whisper.

"You already said that," she replied, watching him smile and lick his lips. She suddenly wished he would lean down and press his gorgeous mouth against hers, the very thought catching her off guard.

"I guess I did say that. You also scare me, Gia." He

brought his hand down to his side and took a step back.

"I scare you? Why?"

It had been way too long since she had feelings for any man, let alone one as handsome and professional as Hartford Parker. The last thing she wanted to do was scare him. Most of the guys she had dated over the years were working stiffs—blue collar guys with no vision or passion for anything; content to work hard during the week and play hard on the weekends. Not that there was anything wrong with it. But Gia was a dreamer—always had been. The only time she honestly felt alive was through the power of dance. The unequivocal sensation that came over her when she moved across a floor was like flying. She was free—free from her worries. Free from her past—and her future. Her body was conditioned to be healthy, the discipline and elegance of her classical training evident in the way she moved. It was her mental conditioning she had to stay on top of, determined to be strong through the constant hard times that had become the norm in her life. If Hart knew how fragile she truly was, he would have good reason to be scared.

"You're beautiful and mysterious. You're also a hard-working, independent woman. It's a rare combination in this day and age, Gia. Not a lot of guys I know could keep up with someone like you." He shifted, putting his hands in his pockets, making his biceps flex.

"I'm not mysterious, Hart. What you see is what you get."

He nodded slightly, his lips tugging at the corners of his mouth as if he were stifling a grin.

In order to change the subject, Gia walked briskly to the middle of the room, gesturing with her arms. "I want your honest opinion. Do you think I should bail like everyone else around here? Or do you think it's worth it to try to keep the business afloat until the tide changes?"

"Until the tide changes? You mean until the area gets a facelift and businesses and families start moving back, living and working in the area again?"

"Yes. What do you think?"

Hart shook his head and ran his hand through his thick hair. "This is your business, Gia. It's your decision. I don't think it's my place to tell you what you should do."

"But do you have any contacts or a way to assess the area? You know, some kind of demographic survey or something to see how the area and the population has changed or if it's getting any better. I know the crime rate has risen, and there are a lot of abandoned and foreclosed homes nearby. With your knowledge and expertise, maybe you could help a girl out?" God knows she didn't want to scare him and come off as needy, but she was desperate to try to figure out her next steps.

"I suppose I could do some research for you, on one condition."

A flicker of hope ignited in her chest as she watched him saunter toward her. "What?"

When he was merely a foot from her, he stopped, his expression soft. "Dance for me," he whispered.

Gia exhaled, aware that her cheeks felt hot.

"Please. Dance for me? Show me what you're passionate about."

She looked up at him, and her breath hitched, knowing she was going to do it. She was going to dance for him. No other man had ever made such a request before. No other man ever really cared that much about her passion. The fact that he politely asked her to reveal her true-self ignited a flame in her belly.

"Okay." She strode toward the door leading to the back of the studio before she changed her mind. "Give me a minute to change. If you could please turn on the stereo and cue the music to track three on the CD, I'd appreciate it." Once she was through the doorway, she palmed the other side of the door and closed her eyes. "I can't believe I'm doing this," she whispered.

Several minutes later, Gia stepped back into the large

37

dance space and gracefully walked to the center of the room. She had changed into a black leotard and jazz pants; her bare feet and pink toenails exposed. Hart was standing next to the sound system, the red "on" light indicating he had the music ready to go. She inhaled deeply and tilted her chin upward with determination. As she exhaled, she offered him a slight nod to show she was ready for him to press play.

The Ed Sheeran song, *Perfect* echoed through the space. Gia closed her eyes and started to move slowly to the music, aware of every delicate motion. She was graceful with each expression in the choreography, her body well-controlled, her muscles flexing, bending, and moving with fluidity all their own—like a breeze billowing a skirt. Each movement was precise, coinciding with the sexy rhythm of the song. She had been working on this piece for weeks, and Hart was the very first to lay eyes on the finished product. What started out as small and concise movement gradually changed to large sweeping gestures as she used the entire space, her whole body involved in the expressive power of the dance.

Gia was wholly engaged in the two-minute piece, ending on the floor with her supple hands reaching toward Hart. Her chest rose and fell as she took in big gulps of air after the strenuous performance, her muscles taut and burning.

He walked quickly toward her and reached with outstretched hands, gripping hers sturdily while hoisting her to her feet. His eyes were wide, and he opened his mouth as if he were about to say something. Instead, he shook his head and pulled her into an embrace, holding her tightly. She panted, wrapping her arms slowly around his waist, not sure what to make of the gesture, his sturdy frame warm and inviting. Finally, he pulled back and slid his hands into her hair before he leaned down and made a trail of kisses across her cheek. Closing her eyes, she rested on him and felt his lips linger against hers, his tongue slipping into the seam of her mouth. She welcomed the kiss that was full of passion and intensity. And she was flying all over again.

GEORGIA ON MY MIND

CHAPTER SIX

Hart was ravenous for Gia, their kiss going from sweet and subtle to spicy and penetrating, her lips and tongue hydrating his soul after the parchedness left behind in his recent drought. He wanted her with every fiber of his being, the growing bulge in his pants evidence of his lustful intentions. Watching her dance was hypnotic, and the experience intoxicated him, never undergoing anything remotely as wanton as he was now. His hands slid down to her buttocks, and he pulled her forward forcefully so she could feel what she had done to him. She grabbed the back of his hair and tugged powerfully, sending a jolt of pain to his scalp.

"Ouch!" he bellowed, stumbling backward. He wiped his mouth with the back of his hand, breathing heavily after the sudden release. Gia stared back at him with a grim expression, making him chastise himself internally for letting his manhood get away from him. He was completely undone and fearful he just fucked it all up.

"I'm sorry, Gia. I crossed a line. It's just that…you're an incredible talent. That dance was… God! It was like watching a bird dive and hurl through the air! You're gorgeous, and you took my breath away with your incredible expression. I couldn't have denied you that embrace or that kiss if I'd wanted to, Gia. I'm so drawn to you and your amazingly beautiful talent." He was muttering like an idiot, trying to backtrack while the two of them stood their ground catching their breath. "Please, Gia." He held his hand out toward her. "Please. I'm sorry. It won't happen again."

He watched her hesitate before offering her hand, his compliments doing the trick. Slowly, he pulled her toward him and gently ran his free hand down her shoulder. "Thank you."

"You're welcome," she replied, her voice husky.

Hart lifted her hand and brought it to his mouth, kissing her knuckles lightly, making her sigh.

"Hart—"

"Gia," he interrupted. "I'll work on the survey for you. Absolutely. But you'll have to forgive me for what just happened. Watching you was magical. I don't know what came over me."

She searched his face with wide eyes, gripping his hand.

"I'm very attracted to you. And that kiss…" He couldn't help but roll his eyes. "Holy shit, that kiss. Please say you'll have dinner with me tonight. I want to make it up to you. I promise I'll stay in control. I won't let that happen again. At least not until you're ready." He offered a dazzling smile. He leaned in and whispered in her ear, "You have more passion in your body than I have in my little finger."

Gia pursed her lips to stifle a giggle, making Hart laugh. "It's true!" He pulled her in for another hug, keeping his hands around her mid-back. "You and me, tonight. What do you say?"

He was shocked when she said, "Okay."

***

Because it was a Monday, Gia didn't have to worry about any students or her staff coming to the studio. As far back as she could remember, the studio had closed on

Sundays and Mondays. She was glad she and Hart had come to a mutual understanding. She was attracted to him and wanted to explore what was next. What that was, she didn't know. All she knew was it felt wonderful to dance like that again with Hartford Parker as her sole audience— to feel the power in her body and to let go of everything, even if it only lasted a couple of minutes. His reaction was the icing on the cake. She wanted to move people with her talent; catch them off guard and leave them breathless. It certainly happened with Hart. The poor guy had come undone, his bold move of grabbing her ass something that probably came naturally to a playboy like him. She had to admit, it would have been easy to get carried away with him. They were both on a high, and if they had succumbed to the physical attraction they had for one another, it wouldn't have been special. And that was what she wanted—something special. It took discipline for her to pull back from his flaming lips and not stroke his hardness. Her body reacted to his touch immediately—her damp panties were proof of that. If only his aggressive passion hadn't scared her, causing her to retreat. She hadn't been intimate with anyone in a very long time and thought it must be just as hard for him to concede, knowing that physically he had been ready and willing to consume her. For him to apologize profusely and immediately offer to take her to dinner was sweet; his invitation genuine.

Hart had agreed to come back around seven and pick her up for their dinner date. She fibbed, telling him she had some work to do in her studio office, not ready to divulge her current living situation. Staring back at her reflection in the small mirror of the only unisex bathroom in her suite, she applied a dab of lip gloss to her full lips. There was no shower or bathtub to speak of in her business, so bathing was a luxury. She made do with her own "sink baths" standing over the old drain in the floor and washing her body using a large sponge. Washing her hair was the most significant challenge, hence the short haircut. When she had first relocated to the studio, her hair was longer, reaching down to her shoulders. After several failed attempts at washing it in the small sink, she got fed up, walked to the nearest haircut chain, and requested something short, radically changing her look. She had to admit, it was a much easier style to maintain—even her wigs for her Marilyn and Madonna gigs fit better. Her life was all about practicality now.

A faint knocking could be heard coming from the front doors. Gia quickly put her lip gloss into a small purse and turned out the lights as she made her way to the entrance. The sun was still shining in the early spring evening as she opened the door, revealing Hartford Parker in a shimmering orb of light.

"Wow!" he stated. "You look gorgeous."

Gia blushed and locked the deadbolt on the door. "Thank you. You look very handsome."

He smiled and offered his bent elbow, escorting her to the passenger side of his Mercedes. He opened the door and gestured his hand in a sweeping motion for her to get in. She erupted in a burst of giggles, aware that he was intentionally showing off his best gentlemanly efforts. When they were both buckled in and on their way, Gia turned toward him. "Thanks again for coming to pick me up."

"You're very welcome. Did you get a lot of work done?" he asked.

Gia quickly nodded. "Yes. There's always a lot to do in the studio." She looked out the window at the foliage that was just starting to bloom. It seemed as if her own heart was opening up, much like the fragile flowering buds on the trees. To be vulnerable and transparent in front of Hart during her dance had been hard, and she knew she had surprised him. He got carried away grabbing her ass and rubbing himself against her, and immediately back-peddled as fast as he could, as if knowing he had made a near-fatal mistake. Clutching her hands nervously in her lap, anticipating the night ahead, she hoped he might be more transparent during dinner and reveal more about himself.

"What are you thinking about?" he asked, looking over at her.

Leaning her head back on the sumptuous leather seat, she turned and admired his masculine features highlighted by the sun. "I'm glad I didn't scare you away."

His smile illuminated his face. "You may have startled me, putting me in my place, but I don't run off so easily."

She matched his smile. "I'm glad."

They arrived at an older country club near the perimeter of the city, the valet service quickly opening their doors. Gia inhaled sharply, disappointment washing over her. She had hoped Hart would take her to dinner at a restaurant in the Buckhead area or the trendy part of Midtown. Old habits must die hard when she realized this was the lifestyle Hart was accustomed to, growing up in an affluent family. She stepped out of the luxury car and waited for him as he tipped the valet and jogged to her side. He must have noticed her demeanor.

"Is this okay?"

Smiling through her nerves, Gia nodded politely and hooked her arm through his.

The hostess sat them at a lovely table by a large window overlooking the golf course, the dipping sun in the sky backlighting the tall Georgia pines and swaths of perfectly manicured grass. They ordered wine, and a perky waitress named Brittany relayed the specials of the evening. A small votive candle flickered in the middle of the table between them and, Gia couldn't help but swoon, looking at the handsome man who sat across from her. He chatted animatedly about his dismal attempts at golf and how it was a necessary evil in the real estate business.

"Thank God I'm as bad as I am. I know I've closed deals based solely on guys feeling sorry for me," he laughed.

Gia took a sip of the expensive wine and savored it. "You said you were in transition now. Are you working at all?"

Hart wiped his mouth with a white linen napkin and cleared his throat. "I'm trying to find my way. I took some time off, and it's been kind of hard getting back in the game."

"Hmm," she answered. "What happened at your last job? Why didn't it work out, if you don't mind me asking?" She was trying to get to know him and was curious as to how his "transition" started.

"It's a long story, Gia." He nervously ran his hand through his hair before taking a big gulp of wine.

Leaning back in her tufted chair, Gia crossed her arms. "Hart, if I can dance in front of you like I did today and thwart off your advances, you can tell me about what happened. I think that's fair."

He chewed on his lip and nodded. "You're tough."

"So are you."

He exhaled. "Okay. You want the truth; you got it."

At first, his story was boastful, explaining his cushy job in DC for a top broker in the nation. He was the "golden boy" of the firm, wining and dining affluent clients and closing million-dollar deals in record timing. He was rubbing elbows with the top one percent of the country. Gia finished her glass of wine, and they shared an appetizer as she listened to his long back story. When their entrees arrived, Hart's countenance changed, and he seemed embarrassed trying to finish the story and explain what had happened.

"It was a black-tie event at the new property located a few blocks from the White House. I was feeling pretty cocky in my tux, prancing around all those big shots, making sure they noticed me. I was the guy who had clinched the deal, bringing in the biggest commission of my life."

Gia set her fork down next to her filet mignon. "What

happened at the event?"

Hart seemed to have lost his appetite. "Let's just say, it didn't go according to plan."

Leaning closer to the table, she tilted her head and pleaded with him. "Please tell me, Hart. I won't judge you. Whatever it is. We all make mistakes in our lives."

His face was pale and his expression morose. He chugged the last bit of wine in his glass before he spoke. "I was caught with my pants down in the client's new office." He swallowed hard. "Literally."

Before Gia could delve further, a loud, condescending baritone voice startled them both.

"Hartford! What a surprise!"

She watched him fumble and stand, his napkin falling to the floor. He seemed to cower under the large man who appeared to be in his retirement years. There was something familiar about him and the petite woman standing a few feet away.

"Hello, Father." He shook the man's hand aggressively.

Gia stood awkwardly waiting for introductions to take place and watched Hart hug the woman he called mother, who was dabbing at her eyes. He quickly came to her side and put his arm around her waist. She wondered if he was holding on to her for support.

"Father? Mother? May I introduce to you, Ms. Gia Bates."

She held out her hand and smiled. "It's a pleasure." The three of them shook hands and exchanged banters.

Mr. Parker puffed out his chest turning toward Hart. "May I have a word with you? In private?"

Hart glanced at Gia and squeezed her waist before whispering in her ear, "I'll only be a moment."

She watched him walk out of the room, trailing his father with his head hanging low, as if in defeat. Whatever happened in DC had obviously spoiled something between them. She'd have to wait a few more minutes before she would get some answers.

GEORGIA ON MY MIND

CHAPTER SEVEN

Hart felt like a chastised child as he walked behind his father into the opulent lobby of the country club, the weeks of avoiding him finally coming to a head. His father stopped near a large potted plant and placed his hands on his hips.

The two eyed each other before Hart nervously spoke. "I'm on a date, Father. What do you want?"

He watched his dad shake his head disappointedly and sigh. "How nice to see you still enjoying the perks of country club living. Have you landed yet? Do you have any news at all? Or are you still freeloading at your sister's condo and charging your dinner tonight to my membership—"

"Stop it, Dad!" he interrupted. "I'll let you know when I've landed so you won't have to be disappointed in me anymore, okay?" He turned to walk away before his father grabbed him by the arm. Hart shook him off and stood his ground. "What do you want from me?"

Mr. Parker grimaced. "I want you to grow up! That's what I want from you. You had it all, Hartford! And you let it all go because you just had to have that rich pussy…"

"*Enough*!" Hart looked around before leaning into the

space between them. "I have more than apologized for my indiscretion. You need to forgive me. Mom has. Katie has. I don't see why you can't either."

"Because you've embarrassed me. You embarrassed our entire family." Mr. Parker's eyes softened. "You had such potential, Hartford. You were a rising star…" He paused and sighed, squeezing the back of his neck. "I'm not sure I can ever get over this."

His heart sank, hearing those words come out of his father's mouth. "Well, then it's your loss." He abruptly turned and walked back toward the dining room, leaving his father standing alone.

His mother intercepted him in the long hallway adorned with stuffy oil paintings and expensive carpet. He hung his head low.

"Hartford." Her smile was full of love. "I'm so glad to see you. And what a lovely date you have tonight. Gia is quite wonderful."

Hart's lips tugged at the corner of his mouth into a half smile. His mother had always been the one constant in his life, never judging or chastising his mistakes. She loved him unconditionally, her adoration something he counted on.

"Thanks, Mom. She is wonderful. I'm so glad you got to meet her."

Mrs. Parker placed her palm on his cheek. "Promise me you'll bring her over for dinner sometime soon." The look on her face was expectant but melancholy, both of them knowing it probably wasn't much of a possibility because of Mr. Parker's unforgiving heart.

"We'll do our best," he said softly, leaning into her touch.

She patted his cheek and nodded sadly. "I love you, Son. You take care."

"Love you too, Mom." He watched her walk away. Taking a deep breath and holding his head high, he reentered the dining room with purpose and approached the table. Gia was gorgeous in the flickering candlelight, holding her refilled wine glass effortlessly with one elbow on the table. Her eyebrow arched as he sat down.

"Sorry about that. I wasn't expecting to see my parents here on a Monday night. They usually come on the weekends." He nervously positioned his napkin back in his lap and cut off a big chunk of steak, shoving it into his mouth. Grinning back at her, he continued to eat and proceeded to pour what was left in the wine bottle into his glass, drinking it greedily.

Gia didn't say a word, and when the waitress came by to check on them, Hart ordered a double Jack Daniels, deciding he needed something stronger than wine to douse his haggard nerves.

"Your mother is nice," Gia said, breaking the uncomfortable silence.

Hart thanked the waitress and took the cocktail from her tray, chugging half of it before replying, "Thanks." The whiskey burned going down his throat, making him wince. He watched her cross her arms and stare at him pensively. "What?"

"Your whole attitude has changed. There's obviously more to the story you haven't finished telling me."

Hart rolled his eyes and collapsed into the back of his chair. "Gia…" he started delicately.

"I saw the way your parents reacted when they saw you here. What did you do, Hart?"

Shaking his head, he avoided her stare and gave up trying to stall for time. He didn't want to spoil the rest of their evening with his sordid tale, but he knew she was tenacious. He decided to forge ahead, ready to get it over with.

"The client's daughter had been flirting with me all night," he said in a low voice, staring at the candle. "We kept celebrating with tequila shots, both of us becoming incredibly tipsy. I was trying to keep things cool, but she took me by the hand and pulled me through the hallway to her father's new office." He glanced at Gia who was listening intently, her blue eyes wide and dark.

"What happened when you got to her father's office?" she asked quietly.

Hart hated reliving the moment his career came to a screeching halt. It made him sick to his stomach. He quickly chugged the remnants of his drink and breathed in through his nose as the ice cubes clinked at the bottom of the empty crystal glass.

"I thought she had locked the door. Her skirt was hiked up, and my pants were down, and I was screwing her like a raging lunatic across her father's twenty-five-thousand-dollar antique desk. We were out-of-our-minds drunk, and before I knew it, a group of people was gasping behind us; her father, *my client* at the forefront of the group." He closed his eyes, remembering the painful moment. "Apparently, he was taking some of the big wigs on a tour of the place."

His head was starting to pound as he stared at Gia from across the table and sighed. "It was the worst, most embarrassing moment of my entire life. I was escorted off the property and promptly let go the next day."

Gia shook her head. "Wow."

"I was arrogant, Gia. I thought I was the king of the world, prancing around like a complete jackass. It didn't take but a split second for me to be brought down into a heaping pile of shit."

He ran his hand through his hair, not caring if he messed it up. His shoulders sagged, and all he wanted to do was retreat to his sister's condo and get drunk—a bad habit he had gotten into for several months that had worried his sister immensely. He should have known better than to come to the country club tonight. The chance encounter with his father made him feel worse. And poor Gia. She had to hear all about his sorry ass and what a fool he'd been. He wouldn't blame her if she never wanted to see him again.

"Come on, let's go." She was standing right next to him with her hand out. He looked up and watched her nod. Tentatively placing his hand on hers, he slowly rose from the chair.

"Do you need to sign the bill or anything?" Her voice was calm and entirely in control.

"No. We're good."

Gia pulled him through the dining room out into the lobby and continued to hold his hand while they waited for the valet to bring the car around.

"Are you okay to drive or do you want me to?" She was looking at him intently, no sign of repulsion or disappointment in her expression at all. The slight buzz from the whiskey had relaxed him, and he knew he was in no position to drive. Without a word, he opened the passenger side door and slid onto the leather seat, ready to lie back and close his eyes.

"Be my guest."

The ride back to her studio didn't take long, and he was surprised when she put the car in park and turned it off right in front.

"Come on," she said, easing her long legs out of the sports car and slamming the door.

Hart wasn't expecting this date to continue, but curiosity got the better of him. He opened the door and pressed the auto-lock button before following her inside the building. He stood with his hands in his pockets and watched her cross the long expanse of the room and put her purse on the piano. "Lock the door," she said.

Hart turned around and latched the deadbolt per Gia's request. When he turned back, *Edge of Desire*, by John Mayer was playing through the speakers, and she was standing in the middle of the room with a smile on her face.

"What are you doing?" he asked. Gia seemed to have a knack for making him nervous.

"Come here."

Hart ran his hand through his hair before slowly ambling toward Gia. He stopped within inches of her, their faces extremely close. Her blue eyes seemed to sparkle in the fluorescent lighting, an indication that she was up to something. He waited with anticipation.

"Give me your left hand." She held her right hand out to her side. Tentatively, he placed his left hand on hers.

"Now put your right hand on my hip."

The way she was looking up at him with those big, blue eyes made his manhood stir. "If you want to dance, just say so. You don't have to be all technical about it," he teased.

Placing his palm on her small waist, he gently pulled her forward to where their bodies were touching. The aroma of her flowery hair was heavenly and immediately infiltrated his nostrils as they started to sway back and forth to the music, the touch of their fingers and the proximity of their bodies releasing noticeable heat. Their chemistry was undeniable, and Hart wasn't sure if he could hold back any longer.

"Why are we dancing, Gia?" he finally asked, his voice raspy with desire.

She looked up into his face, her expression soft but etched with concern. "You were pretty stressed out. I find that dancing always calms me down, so I thought it might do the same for you."

"Hmmm," he mumbled, unaccustomed to the kindness she was displaying. He leaned in and rested his chin on her head, closing his eyes. He was finally starting to unwind since arriving at the studio. Warm, soft lips touched his jawline, surprising him, and he immediately tensed.

"Shh," she whispered, her warm breath floating over his skin. "Relax, Hart."

He slid his left hand down her side, wrapped his arms around her waist, and buried his face into the sweet crevice of her neck. She snuggled into his embrace, and they continued to dance, neither one of them realizing the song had ended until she started to giggle.

"What?"

"The music stopped."

"That doesn't mean we have to." Hart pulled back and brought his hands up to hold her face gently with his large palms. Her pupils dilated with want, the pale blueness of her incredible eyes obscured. "Can I kiss you? Please?" His brow creased as he patiently waited for her to answer.

"Yes."

He started to move in, but she put her hand up to his mouth, stopping him in his tracks.

"Before you do, you need to know that I'm glad you told me the truth."

"You are?"

"Yes. I know it was hard. And I know you've been through a lot, even if you did bring it upon yourself."

Hart shook his head and looked at the floor. She grabbed his chin, forcing him to look at her. "I know what it's like to want to give up."

Her face was filled with empathy. He stared at her, not knowing how to respond. He didn't have to. Gia leaned in and covered his mouth with hers, their tongues exploding in a frenzy of want and need. The guilt he felt about his scandalous past just seconds earlier shattered when her lips melded with his. It was as if a hammer slammed through a large plate of glass, the shards bursting through the air, the noise deafening, leaving him reeling in her arms.

GEORGIA ON MY MIND

CHAPTER EIGHT

Gia didn't want to cave. She didn't want to give herself up entirely to Hart on their first official date, especially learning the truth about what he had done. But there was something different about the way she felt when she was with this man—it was carnal and primitive, and she couldn't hold back any longer. His hands gripped her lower back as if he were holding on for dear life, his kiss consuming her. Her fingertips tugged on his hair, and she couldn't help but bend one of her long legs and bring it up, brushing against his outer thigh.

"I want you Gia. You gotta know that. I wasn't expecting this, especially after telling you my story. Tell me to stop now…if you want me to."

Hart's voice was low and rumbling, his hot breath on her exposed neck causing her skin to prickle with goosebumps. She pulled back and licked her swollen lips, staring into his chocolate eyes. He took his index finger and gently swiped it across her forehead, moving her bangs to the side.

"Hold that thought," she whispered. Quickly, she walked to the bank of lights by the front door and turned off the overhead fluorescents. They were in the dark for a second before she flicked the switch on another panel and a spotlight shown on a small disco ball that started to turn in the center of the ceiling. Subtle orbs of light showered the room, like stars falling across a dark sky.

The smile that blossomed across Hart's face as he looked around the room with pleasure caused her heart to skip a beat. He was gorgeous. And he was flawed—a definite Southern playboy who had probably been with many, many women over the years. Was she willing to give herself up to his advances? He openly admitted that he had put himself into a self-induced time-out from the dating scene for several months. Was he genuinely attracted to her or was he just horny and ready to jump back on the flavor-of-the-month bandwagon? And did it matter? His flavor was tasting really good to her right now.

She approached the sound system and put in a random CD of classical music. The haunting melody of Rachmaninoff's, *Rhapsody on a Theme of Paganini* started to play, making her smile. It was utterly romantic and soft; the perfect choice to explore the Hart of Dixie. Slowly and intentionally, she approached him, the two of them standing in the center of the studio with the shower of light spinning around them. Hart reached his hand up to her cheek and pushed her hair over her ear, his hand lingering on the side of her head.

"This piece is beautiful. Like you," he uttered.

Gia's cheeks grew hot and she couldn't help but smile. Boldly, she wrapped her arms around him and lay her head against his chest, listening to the faintest sound of his heart beating. His solid arms held her close, and she felt safe for the first time in years. He leaned down, and they kissed. At first, it was gentle and soft, his moist lips and tongue nipping and teasing her mouth. As their kissing intensified, they groped each other and moved across the floor to the ballet barre.

"Turn around," Hart gruffly whispered.

She turned and placed her hands on the well-worn

wood of the barre and stared at his reflection behind her in the wall of mirrors. His eyes were wide and dark, his hair tousled, as if he had just gotten out of bed.

"Look at yourself, Gia. You're so beautiful and mysterious. I've never met anyone like you."

Gia laughed. "I'll bet you say that to all your dates."

His brow furrowed as he leaned his chin on her shoulder. "Seriously. Look at yourself. You're drop-dead gorgeous. Just watch."

He wrapped one of his arms around her waist and pulled her snuggly against his body, his hardness obvious. Using his other hand, he tenderly caressed her tummy, making her shiver with desire. Slowly, his palm glided up to her breasts, his fingertips on the outside of her clothing sending electric shock waves throughout her body.

She gripped the barre and tensed, the sensation of a man's hands on her something she hadn't felt in a very long time. With wide eyes, she watched him as one hand squeezed her breast, and the other slithered its way down to her crotch and rubbed against the outside of her skirt. She inhaled sharply, her tingling insides making her shudder. Her head rolled back against his chest, and his lips softly dragged over the delicate skin of her neck.

The music changed to the upbeat Mozart, *Piano Sonata in C*, immediately bringing to mind visions of her tiniest ballet students scurrying across the floor. She couldn't help but giggle.

"Am I tickling you?" Hart asked, smiling into her neck.

"No…it feels wonderful." She reached up and ran one hand through his hair, rolling her neck as he continued to kiss and fondle her.

He stepped back and unzipped the back of her black skirt, his eyes locked in on hers in the reflection of the mirror. Breathless, she pulled her soft sweater up and over her head and stepped out of the skirt that pooled at her heeled feet on the floor.

"Keep your heels on," he insisted. "And put both

hands back on the barre."

Her chest was rising and falling as she gripped the wood. Leaning his solid body against her, he ran his hands over her exposed skin.

"Spread your legs and bend over slightly," he requested. His chest was rising and falling too as he quietly instructed her.

Slowly, she took two steps away from the barre, pushing against his noticeable bulge and bent over slightly, raising her butt in the air. Hart continued to run his hand around her waist down to her underwear, his curious fingers lifting the garment and sliding down to her soft mound. She whimpered as his index finger brushed her swollen clit, teasing her mercilessly while grinding his crotch against her ass.

"You feel…amazing," he gasped. "Just look at how beautiful your reflection is." He paused, and she watched him bite his lip sensually. "I want to watch you come undone in the mirror."

She couldn't help but look at herself, the image of her and Hart sexy and stimulating. Her body gyrated against his hand that was down her panties, his other grasping at her exposed breast, the strap of her bra hanging limply across her arm. The fast-moving piano piece and the swirling lights added to the roller-coaster ride that was her fast approaching orgasm. Before she could utter a word, Hart forcefully turned her around to face him and swiftly pulled down her panties as he dropped to his knees.

"Hold on," he exhaled before gripping her buttocks with his hands and planting his face into her crotch.

"Oh, my god!" Gia gripped the barre and couldn't help but spread her legs wide, the sensation of his lips and tongue teasing and pulling on her most sensitive area overwhelming. She inhaled quickly with her mouth wide open, and her head rolled back as she tensed and shut her eyes tightly. A warmth of moisture surged throughout her abdomen causing her to shudder uncontrollably.

"*Hart!*" she cried out, grasping the wooden barre and holding on for dear life.

His grip on her butt cheeks intensified as he tasted every ounce of her pleasure. Her head was swirling, and her body convulsed before she lost her hold on the barre. She could barely make out Hart standing swiftly and catching her as she collapsed into his arms. The lights continued to pulse, and she closed her eyes again, the piano music changing to something more subdued.

"You're trembling," Hart whispered into her ear, clutching her against his chest.

She held him tightly around his waist and concentrated on her breathing—in and out, in and out. It took several minutes before she came down from the intense experience of a Hartford Parker orgasm. He seemed to sense she was more relaxed and pulled back, reaching down to the floor and delicately pulling her panties back up and over her bare private area.

"Thank you," she managed to say while pulling her bra strap up and adjusting the C-cup to cover her breast. Biting her lower lip, she finally managed to look him in the eye. "That was… incredible."

His eyes seemed to shine in the light as he smiled back at her. "You're incredible." She watched him gather her clothing from the floor.

"Wait. What about you?" she asked, taking her clothes from his hands.

"No." He shook his head, gazing back at her, his smile subdued. "This was all about you tonight. I don't want to push my luck."

"Wait. What?" Confusion flooded her, the onset of panic immediate. Perhaps he wasn't as attracted to her as she thought. She watched him walk across the dance floor to the stereo and turn it off. As he approached her in the silence of the starry room, she couldn't help but be disappointed that their sexual encounter had ended.

"Put your clothes back on. I need to use your

bathroom. Is it back there?" He pointed to the door in the corner.

Gia could only nod, further disappointment creeping into her being. He kissed her lightly on the cheek before walking away.

Shrugging on her sweater, she could feel tears brimming in her eyes. She stepped into her skirt, zipping it quickly in the back and looked at her reflection in the mirror, patting her messy hair back into place. Her heels clicked across the floor as she approached the panel of lights and turned off the disco ball, the fluorescent bulbs buzzing and popping as they came back on, the harshness of the light making her squint. When Hart returned, his beaming smile melted her heart. He reached his hand out and pulled her to his side.

"Grab your purse. I'll walk you to your car."

She nodded forlornly.

When they were outside in the brisk night air, she leaned against the door of her car and drank in the image of Hartford as he stood in front of her, caressing her face with his thumbs. She didn't want the night to end.

"I don't understand. You don't want me to please you?" She boldly asked the question that had been on the tip of her tongue since the last quiver of her orgasm.

Hart shook his head. "Not tonight. Not after I told you the most embarrassing story of my life. That would have made this entire evening cliché."

She was confused. "What do you mean?"

His hands ran down her arms to her fingertips, and he raised one of her hands to his mouth, kissing her skin. "I'm not that guy, Gia. Whether you believe me or not, I promise you; I don't go to bed with every beautiful woman I meet."

"Okay…"

"There'll be plenty of time for my pleasure. I'd rather wait and have that special moment with you when my past doesn't shadow it. Right now, I'm more concerned about pleasing you." He tilted his head and grinned. "How are you feeling right now?"

Heat infused her cheeks again. "Fantastic. Relaxed."

"Good. Mission accomplished." He pulled her in for another hug, pushing her hair away from her ear. "I want to see you again. As soon as possible, if you'll let me." His breath was warm and intoxicating.

"I would love that."

Hart grabbed both of her cheeks and planted a swift, wet kiss on her mouth, leaving her reeling. "I really need to go, Gia, or I'm not gonna make it home tonight. I'll call you in the morning." He kissed her again before pulling away with a lingering smile on his moist lips.

Sliding into the front seat, she looked up at him. "Good night, Hart."

"Good night, sweet thing." He winked and shut the door, sending her into a swoon.

GEORGIA ON MY MIND

CHAPTER NINE

Hart waited until Gia pulled out of the parking lot and watched the taillights of her car fade into the black night as she drove off in the opposite direction he was going. It amazed him that he was able to muster the willpower to restrain himself from making love to her that night, his enduring boner an indication of what he was up against. She was captivating and good god, so sweet and delicious. He brought his fingertips up to his nose and inhaled the lingering scent of her secret garden. It would have been easy to have pulled down his pants and impaled her sweetness from behind, watching their reflections come undone together. But what he told her was true. He wasn't that guy—not anymore. He made up his mind to only please her and was entranced at how her body responded to his touch. The anticipation of lying with her would gnaw at him, for sure. But he was determined to be the gentleman he claimed he was. She deserved to be pursued and courted, not man-handled and ogled like the men at her entertainment job.

When he pulled into the parking space in front of his sister's condo, he couldn't help but grab his phone and text her.

Thank you for the fantastic night—and for listening and not judging me too harshly.

He waited a few seconds before her response lit up his face in the interior of his car.

I'm the one who should be thanking you!

He chuckled at the blushing emoji face she included.

Sweet dreams, sweet thing. I'll call you tomorrow.

He smiled when she texted back.

I can't wait.

*

Gia lay in the dark on the couch in her storage room, the afterglow of the evening with Hart making her smile. Just thinking about his hands and mouth all over her body under the disco ball in the studio caused her heart to flutter with want. It was astonishing he could hold back from his own needs, wanting only to please her. If he was trying to prove his gentleman status, he succeeded.

When they left the studio, she drove around the block, checking her rearview mirror to make sure he wasn't following. When the coast was clear, she returned and parked in front of her studio and scurried inside, deadbolting the lock for the night. Hart's transparency was noble, and she couldn't help but feel guilty for not coming clean about her living conditions. What he didn't know wouldn't hurt him, right? She didn't want him to know. She'd find a way out of her predicament if she had to work night and day to do it.

Sighing in the dark, she ran her hand up the inside of her t-shirt and fondled her breast, visions of Hart's hands on her body coming to mind. The way he turned her around to face the mirror and watch her image as he brought her to ecstasy was thrilling and sexy. He was sexy, and she wanted more. The storage closet couch-bed was not an option. She'd have to navigate her secret carefully and insist they make love for the first time at his place. Or his sister's home—whatever he called it. Relaxed and in total bliss, Gia slowly nodded off, imagining Hart lying next to her.

The next morning came quickly, and a pounding sound coming from the front door startled Gia out of a deep sleep. She grabbed yoga pants off the chair and stepped into flip-flops by the door. Latching the storage room tight behind her, she ran to the front of the studio, patting her hair down.

"Who is it?" she yelled. It was still relatively early, her first students of the day not arriving until after lunch.

"Miss Gia, it's Edward."

Gia sighed, her shoulders immediately sagging. Taking a deep breath and plastering a smile on her face, she opened the door.

"Good morning, Edward. You're up bright and early!"

"I saw your car in the lot and knew you were here, so I thought I'd stop by and get your rent. It's five days past due, Miss Gia."

Edward Smith was an elderly gentleman who had owned the strip mall for as long as she could remember. He was kind and compassionate; always a bit embarrassed coming to Gia month after month to pick up the continually tardy rent check. She was the one who should be embarrassed being late all the time. The old man stood before her, clutching his well-worn ball cap in his gnarled hands.

"You want to come in for some coffee? I…I've been getting some work done this morning and could use some myself."

"No ma'am, I've had my share this morning. Just here for the rent."

Gia pursed her lips. "I was out late last night on a gig. I'm picking up the check this morning and will get it deposited right away. I'll have your rent check before lunch. Sound good?" She held her breath and watched Edward nod bashfully before putting his ball cap over his thinning, gray hair.

"Sounds good. I'll see you in a bit."

"Okay. Bye!" She shut the door and bolted the lock. "Fuck," she cursed under her breath.

The check the entertainment company owed her plus what little she already had in the bank would barely cover her rent, leaving next to nothing left over. She still had her staff to pay, and the one credit card she had was maxed out. She was out of options as the two banks she'd visited the previous week had turned her down for a small business loan. Her head started to throb as she plodded back to her living quarters to get dressed for the day ahead.

By the time she reached the windowless, free-standing white stucco building off Highway 141 aptly named *The White Satin*, Gia had formulated a plan in her mind. She needed money and was willing to pay interest on a small loan from the owner, Franko Bartelli. She had purposefully worn her highest heels and a tight, knit dress that accentuated every lean curve on her body. Her black hair was flat-ironed to perfection, and her lips painted in a flashy red. Laughing at her reflection in the wall of mirrors back at her studio, she realized she looked like she just stepped out of a 1940s mobster movie. Hopefully, New York born and raised Franko would approve and have it in his heart to loan her the money.

The strip club wasn't open for business until happy hour, but the side doors were spread wide, allowing liquor vendors to roll in boxes of alcohol from their trucks covered in brightly colored pictures, advertising the latest vodka and bourbon flavors. Several men whistled loudly, liking what they saw. Ignoring them, she walked into the building with purpose and blinked several times as she tried to adjust to the dim interior. The space smelled faintly of old cigars and stale beer. The focal point of the room was a large stage embellished with heavy, red velvet curtains and a gold-trimmed proscenium. The entire space was a throwback to an era from long ago. If the owner hadn't made the place into a strip club, Gia thought it could have been a trendy jazz club or perhaps a local dinner theater. She marched toward the large management office off the lobby that was dripping with gold sconces and marble floors, the opulence obvious.

"Knock-knock! It's Gia Bates." She pushed the door open, peeking inside. Franko had reading glasses on and quickly pulled them off, arching his eyebrow in surprise. He was impeccably dressed in a suit and red satin tie and wore a large gold ring with a significant diamond on his pinky finger.

"Georgia B.! So good to see you on this beautiful spring day!" He came from around his desk and held his arms out to hug her. She didn't refuse. "And looking all sexy and glamorous too, I might add! What's the occasion, Georgia?" His New York accent was broad and loud.

Gia hated it that he called her by her birth name, Georgia. It was her legal name on her driver's license, and unfortunately, on her checks Franko personally wrote out to her. She had shortened her name to "Gia" many years ago after a significant life-altering event. Unfortunately, unless she legally changed her name, it would remain the same on her license.

"I'm here for my monthly check. If I'm not mistaken, I performed five Marilyn acts, three Madonna's and two Officer Good Body. I've got the calendar printout right here." She started to pull a piece of paper out of her purse.

"Nah, I don't need that." Sitting in his office chair, he pulled out and opened a large, leather-bound book and scribbled on a check with his expensive gold pen. "That should do it." With a full grin, he ripped the check out of the book and handed it to her.

Right away, Gia noticed he had added one-hundred dollars to the original total, making her eyes light up. "Thanks, Franko! What did I do to deserve the big tip?"

Franko rose from his chair and came around to the front of the desk where he leaned his butt and crossed his arms. "You look too damn good today for me not to give you a tip, Georgia B."

Shaking her head, Gia quickly put the check in her purse.

"Seriously, when are you gonna come work for me at the club? You'd be such a big hit! You're stunning and sexy as hell…" He pointed his finger directly at her. "I could see you doin' a number from that musical, *Chicago*. You know, bring a little theatrics into the joint with your dance training and all. You even look like that gal from the movie too. You know, the dark-haired one."

"Catherine Zeta-Jones? She played Velma."

"Yeah! That's the one. Man, you'd bring the house down with a Velma act." He eyed her up and down while nodding. "I've always told you, I'd make it worth your while."

Gia stood tall and offered him her most seductive smile. "I appreciate that, Franko. You've always been very complimentary and respectful." She took in a deep breath. "There is something I wanted to ask you."

"Oh, yeah? What's that, Georgia B.?" He leaned back with his palms on the desk.

"I need a favor. A small loan—two-thousand dollars. I'm willing to pay interest on it until I can pay you back. You can also book me as Marilyn or Madonna every night this month if you want to."

He scowled, interrupting her. "Geez, Georgia. You in some kind of trouble? You need help?"

She quickly shook her head. "No, no it's nothing like that. My business…my dance studio is challenging at the moment. I need to get some bills paid and figure out my next steps. Two-thousand dollars is all I'm asking. I would appreciate it more than you know."

"Hmmm…" He stood and sucked in his expanding middle, placing his hands on his hips. "You know, you could make two-thousand dollars outright in one weekend here at the club. You would owe me nothin'—no interest either. All tips are yours too. Some of my gals have made up to five-grand in a weekend. Something to consider."

Gia's heart fell. "So, you won't give me the loan?"

Franko smirked. "How's about I guarantee you two-grand this Friday night." He held up two stubby fingers, his pinky ring flashing in the light. "Two shows. No strings attached. If you like it, the job is yours. Whadyasay?"

"I…I don't know, Franko. You know I'm not comfortable with the idea of being naked in front of a bunch of strangers. I mean, in my Marilyn and Madonna acts I purposefully wear beautiful undergarments to give an illusion rather than going all the way." She nervously clutched her purse with both hands, realizing asking Franko Bartelli for money wasn't such a good idea.

He filled the space that was between them and held up two fingers again. "Two shows. I'll even put you in the prime 11:30 slot." He brushed his calloused index finger quickly across her lips. "Think about it."

CHAPTER TEN

Hart caught himself whistling while rinsing out a coffee pot in his sister's galley-kitchen. He couldn't help but grin and shake his head, thoughts of Gia Bates coming to mind. And he was on a mission to help her out of the crumbling real estate her business resided in.

Up at the crack of dawn, he had showered and shaved as if he were leaving for an office. Dressed casually, he set up his laptop on the dining room table and did some research. The address of Dance Atlanta was in a bad part of town. The crime rate was through the roof, and the resale market of neighboring homes was pitiful, the rate of foreclosures staggering. After a few phone calls to some of his Atlanta brokerage contacts, he was able to find out that the owner of the strip mall was an elderly man named Edward Smith. He had developed the site back in the early 80s and still ran the property without a management company. Hart believed his father might very well know Mr. Smith from back in his real estate days. If only he could talk to his dad about it—get his take on the situation. He'd probably tell Hart the same thing he was thinking—the building was toast and needed to be razed to make room for new development. Mixed-use developments were all the rage nowadays featuring twelve-screen movie theaters, Class-A office space, retail space and luxury level residences, all with the promise of resort-level hospitality. He could picture Gia in a new space with exceptional amenities, her studio flourishing just like the old days. Of course, Mr. Smith would have to agree to sell, and then there would be bids for a developer and a construction company. This would only happen if the Atlanta City Council even approved the project in the first place.

Hart's head was swimming with ideas, and he had to laugh at his presumptuous tendencies. He was in no way, shape or form even close to taking on a project this huge without being employed. Sure, he had ample savings and stock investments. But a project this big would need significant backing from a reputable firm. Hart had always been an ace in the business, bringing considerable deals to the table, his ideas and implementation highly sought after—until his embarrassing transgression in DC. He scratched his head, trying to think of someone in his business that might take a chance on him and his pipe dream. He was still an ace and just needed to prove himself. Mr. Smith's property might just be his ticket to getting him back in the game.

Remembering he had snapped a photo of a dilapidated lease sign in front of the strip mall, Hart pulled out his phone and dialed the number. After two rings, a male voice answered.

"Hello?"

"Good morning. Is this Mr. Smith?"

"Speaking."

"Hey, Mr. Smith. My name is Hartford Parker. I'm a friend of Gia Bates. She told me all about your property and the vacancies you currently have. I'm a real-estate broker in Atlanta, and I'd love to speak with you sometime soon. Perhaps we could meet at the diner over a cup of coffee?"

Hart waited with anticipation for Mr. Smith's response.

"You're the first person to call this number in months. I'd be happy to meet with you at the diner, but only if it includes pie. They make the best pie."

Hart laughed out loud. "Thank you, Mr. Smith! Pie it is!"

***

Hart sat in the same corner booth he and Gia had shared the day before, waiting for Mr. Smith, when Angel approached him.

"Well, look who's back. How you doin' Mr. Hart?"

He was impressed she remembered his name. "I'm fine. How are you today, Angel?"

"Can't complain. You just missed Gia. She was in here for lunch before her first class of the day. Are you late to meet her?"

"No, ma'am. I'll see her later. I'm meeting with Mr. Edward Smith. Do you know him?"

Angel's eyes widened, and she cocked her head in surprise. "Do I know him? He's the most regular customer I have. He owns this place."

Hart chuckled and nodded. "Yes. I have a meeting with him, and he suggested pie."

Angel smiled knowingly. "Yes. Ed loves his pie. He's gonna be especially happy when I tell him it's lemon meringue today." She held up the menus in her hand. "Will you be needin' these?"

"Nah. But I will take some of that delicious sweet tea while I'm waiting for him."

"You got it."

Hart didn't have any notes with him, nor was he dressed-for-success in his usual three-piece suit and tie. He didn't want to intimidate the old man and opted for a collared shirt and khaki pants, appropriate casual business attire for the occasion. Sipping on his iced tea, Hart looked out the plate-glass window at the Dance Atlanta studio across the empty parking lot and wondered what Gia was up to inside. Not wanting to get her hopes up, he hadn't called or texted about his meeting with Mr. Smith. Due diligence was necessary at the forefront of opportunity, and that was what he was doing. If anything of consequence came of his meeting today, he'd let her know about it.

"Mr. Parker?"

Hart looked up and slipped across the bench to stand. "Mr. Smith! It's a pleasure to meet you."

"Please don't stand on my account." The two shook hands before Mr. Smith slid onto the booth bench across from him.

Before the two of them could start a conversation, Angel was beside the table, turning a mug upright and filling it with coffee from a silver pot. "Ed, don't you ever get tired of me?" she teased, setting a handful of small creamers next to his cup.

The old man snickered. "You know this is my favorite place to come for pie."

"And cheeseburgers, and chicken-fried-steak, and meatloaf…"

Hart laughed, watching the two of them banter back and forth.

"I'll get y'all hooked up with two slices of the lemon meringue."

Mr. Smith rubbed his palms together with glee before leaning toward Hart across the table. "It's real meringue too, none of that store-bought crap."

He nodded and took a sip of his tea.

"So, you're a friend of Georgia's, huh?"

His question startled Hart. "You mean, Gia, right?"

Ed rolled his eyes. "Yeah. She gets on to me for still calling her by her birth name. I've told her to cut me some slack 'cause I'm old and that's what I called her when she was growing up." The elderly man sipped the hot coffee carefully.

Hart tried not to act too surprised, clearing his throat.

"I'm a new friend of Gia's. We only met just last week. She's quite something."

Ed nodded in agreement. "Yep. Her late Aunt Caroline was the original owner of the dance studio. She was a terrific influence on her when she went through a bunch of stuff as a kid."

Shifting in his seat, Hart wasn't prepared for small talk about Gia. But he was intrigued and wanted to know more. "So, you've known her for a while?"

"Her entire life. She was the cutest little thing, riding her bike to dance class, wearing a pink tutu and ballet slippers. Dancing has always been her passion, keeping her out of trouble, unlike that no-good mama of hers."

Hearing the old man dis Gia's mother surprised Hart and he cleared his throat. "Yes, she's quite a good dancer."

"You've seen her dance?" The old man looked at him expectantly.

"Umm…" Hart wasn't sure how to explain the solo performance Gia had done just for him the day before. "Yes. I have." He left it at that.

"Well, I hope she can make ends meet. I know it hasn't been easy for her these last few months. She had to let most of her staff go."

"Yes, I know."

"She sure tries. I hope it pans out, but if you want to know the truth, I think she'd be better off letting her lease run out and relocate somewhere else; somewhere nice and safe. You know, a place with lots of young families with children. There ain't many kids around these parts anymore."

Angel dropped off two giant pieces of pie topped with at least six inches of creamy meringue. "Y'all enjoy," she said, grinning from ear to ear.

Hart's eyes almost popped out of his head. He could eat his fair share of donuts, but there was no way he could eat a piece of a pie that large without getting a severe sugar headache. Mr. Smith was already diving into his, happily munching away.

"You wanna talk real estate?" he asked with his mouth full.

"Yes, sir. That's why I called and wanted to meet."

Mr. Smith nodded. "I'll give you the low-down real quick." He wiped his face with a paper napkin. "I've been running this little corner of Atlanta since 1981. We've had our highs and our lows over the years. I thought about selling in the mid-nineties but wasn't quite ready. Then the recession hit. I haven't been the same since."

Hart nodded empathetically while taking tiny bites of pie.

"No one is even interested in buying now. The area has gone to crap; crime everywhere and no one leasing space—at least, anyone reputable. I could lease to a bunch of pawn shops and title loan sharks, but I haven't stooped to that level yet. But if I keep losing my tenants, I may have to suck it up for the revenue."

"Have you ever thought about improvements? Maybe a giant facelift? Asking the county for tax incentives for new tenants?"

"Been there, done that, son. Banks won't loan me the money for the kind of renovations I need." He took a big bite of pie and let the conversation breathe. "Don't get me wrong; there's still a lot of good folks around here. Our area just happens to have fallen into that dark hole of the recession, and we haven't quite figured out how to climb out of it. It's slow goin', that's for sure. But the tide will eventually change, if I live to see the day."

Hart pushed his half-eaten pie to the side. "If I could get some people on board to take a look at your property, maybe come up with a few ideas, would you be willing?"

Mr. Smith blew a puff of air out his nostrils. "Sure. At this point, I'm willing to look at hiring a hitman to torch the place for the insurance money."

Hart laughed out loud. "Hopefully, it won't come down to that Mr. Smith. And I'm pretty sure they don't serve lemon meringue pie in prison."

GEORGIA ON MY MIND

CHAPTER ELEVEN

Gia shook her head disappointedly; only four students in her three-to-five-year-old class. Four. Back in the day, she would have had ten to twelve, easily, the studio space frolicking with small humans dressed in pink among giggles and music. She held her head high, knowing it didn't matter if she had one student or one hundred; she would teach the class with enthusiasm and professionalism. These little girls looked up to her, and she wasn't about to let them down. She was also indebted to their parents who still brought their little ones to this side of town for basic ballet training.

The mothers sat in folding chairs against the wall opposite the mirrors, fixated on their smartphones as Gia began the class. She had the girls form a circle, hold hands, and sit. When they were situated, she stretched her long legs out.

"Legs straight out. Let's warm up our feet, okay? First, we flex our feet and say 'hello' to our toes."

The little girls giggled following Gia intently.

"Now we point our feet and say 'goodbye' toes." She pointed her seasoned ballerina feet toward the middle of the circle, the fundamental warm-up repeated several times

81

before they raised their hands into the air reaching for imaginary stars.

As Gia raised her long arms toward the ceiling, she spotted the small disco ball and remembered the twinkling lights that had swirled in this very space, blushing with the memory. She recalled Hart's gorgeous face among the colored orbs, his strong jawline, and full lips unforgettable. And what he did with his mouth...

"Let's stretch our hips now. We've got jelly on the bottom of one foot and peanut butter on the bottom of the other. Let's make a sandwich!" Pressing the bottoms of her feet together, she showed the girls how to rock back and forth with their soles planted together. Her concentration was way off as she rolled her hips, aware of her tingling insides.

Getting the girls up on their feet, they practiced hopping like bunnies across the space before doing their favorite—the princess walk. She encouraged them to walk on their toes with their heads held high carrying an imaginary princess crown.

"Don't look down or your beautiful crown will fall off!"

The last warm-up was skipping, Gia showing them how to pick up their feet as they frolicked across the room. The exercises were essential elements of dance, helping each child with their motor skills. After a few passes back and forth across the expansive room, she had everyone use their imagination and play follow-the-leader, pretending to be wild animals leaping over streams and crawling under trees. The girls loved it, purring and growling in between their young laughter. Gia finally had them move right up to the ballet barre and got them settled into first position.

"That's it. Bend your knees and keep your feet on the ground. Pretend like your little heels are kissing." She walked by each student, slightly adjusting their tiny bodies, thinking about the kisses she'd received the night before.

As the class continued, her students practiced pliés and

passés, bending their tiny bodies into basic ballet positions, all to the proud satisfaction of their mothers who looked on. The door to the studio opened, and Gia almost gasped out loud when she realized it was Hart who had entered. He offered her a gorgeous smile and waved, making her heart leap in her chest like a prima ballerina performing a grand jeté across a stage. She watched him politely say hello to the seated women who were looking him up and down with slight smirks on their faces before he sat in a folding chair next to them. The class was almost over, the little girls anticipating their favorite part of the hour— freeze dance.

Gia clapped her hands while walking briskly over to the sound system. "Okay, okay! Time for our favorite game before I pass out the stickers." She turned on the classic Disney tune, *Let It Go* and encouraged the girls to dance however they pleased. She joined them, twirling and leaping, all the while glancing shyly at Hart who had a perpetual grin plastered across his face. Little girls grabbed her hands, pulling her around the room, taking turns twisting and swinging their arms. Gia loved engaging with her students, who were uninhibited by anything else during her time with them, totally focused on dance, lost in a moment of pure joy.

When the last note of the song played, the girls squealed and hugged Gia's long legs tightly, showering her with affection. She patted their tiny buns while looking over at Hart, who was now standing with his hands on his hips, watching her every move as the mothers around him gathered their things. Two of the moms approached her with checks. She thanked them profusely, politely reminding them of the next class. Grabbing a basket of an assortment of pretty princess and ballerina stickers, each little girl eagerly chose a prize and politely thanked Gia before heading out the door.

Hart came toward her, the look on his face magnetic. She held up a Cinderella sticker. "Would you like a sticker too?" she asked sweetly.

His eyes were bright as he nodded. "Sure. What do you think would go best with my white shirt?" He was playful, and she loved every minute of it.

"Hmm. I think I have a Prince Charming in here somewhere…" She sifted through the basket until she found the sticker she was looking for. "Yep. This is perfect." She held the sticker out for him and watched the sides of his mouth turn up into a broad smile.

"Prince Charming, huh? You set your sights high." He peeled the backing off the sticker before placing it over his heart.

"Yes, I do." She placed the basket on top of the piano. "What brings you out here today?" She was curious as to why he stopped by—and excited. For him to take time out of his day to check in on her was thrilling.

"Bye, Gia!"

Hart and Gia turned toward the door, both of them waving. "Bye!"

As the door shut and they were finally alone, she turned back to Hart and smiled. "Alone at last. Seriously, why are you here?"

He brought his hands up to her bare arms and ran them the length of her exposed skin. She couldn't help but lean into his touch.

"I was in the area and had to see you again. By the way, you look sexy in this outfit."

Her eyebrows rose as she looked down at herself, dressed in her standard ballet wear of pink tights and slippers, black leotard, and a short, black dance skirt tied at the hip.

"It's my uniform," she teased, looking back up at him through her lashes.

Licking his lips, he brought his thumb up to her mouth and gently rubbed it across her lower lip. Her eyes were fixated on his while she listened to the inner voice in her head screaming, "*Kiss me! Kiss me!*"

"What's going through your mind at this exact moment?" he asked.

Gia exhaled and replied honestly, "I want you to kiss me."

"You do?"

"Yes."

He took a step forward, filling the space between them, and cupped her face with his hands. "Your wish is granted," he whispered with a reserved smile, his expression playful as he slowly leaned down and covered her mouth with his.

Gia wrapped her arms around his sturdy frame and welcomed him in. She felt as though she was spinning and twirling among the clouds in the sky. A male voice cleared his throat, startling the two of them out of their embrace.

"Ethan! You scared me!" She quickly stepped back from Hart. "How long have you been in here?"

"Long enough," he answered, grinning largely. "Who's your friend?"

Gia was aware her face and neck were on fire, her skin probably an embarrassing color of a ripe tomato.

"I'm Hart. Nice to meet you, Ethan."

The two men shook hands.

"Likewise. I'm one of the instructors here at the studio."

By this time, Gia had gathered her wits and stood tall next to Hart, pushing her hair over her ear. "Ethan teaches the four o'clock tap class. He's amazing."

"Thanks, Gia." He eyed Hart. "You look like you could be a tapper. Ever tried?"

Hart seemed taken aback. "Who? Me? No way. My version of dancing is the white man over-bite." He moved his head to an imaginary beat while biting his lower lip, making Ethan laugh out loud.

"That's funny, man. I'm gonna remember that." He shifted the black tap shoes in his arms. "Gia, may I have a word with you in the breakroom before class starts?"

"Sure." She turned to Hart, lightly touching his hand with her fingers. "I'll be right back."

"Okay. Nice to meet you, Ethan."

"You too, man."

By the time they got into the breakroom, Gia was pursing her lips to keep from smiling, well aware that Ethan was on her tail.

"Good, god! Where did you meet him?" Ethan had always been an openly gay man. He was uber-talented and often sought after by the local equity theaters to choreograph shows. His love life was an open book, the two of them often commiserating about their horrific dating lives, cheering each other on to ultimately finding true love.

She poked her head around the corner to make sure Hart was out of earshot. "Shhh. Keep your voice down. He can hear us."

"Seriously, Gia. When did you start dating someone? I've known you forever, and you haven't told me anything about this guy. Where'd you meet?"

She pulled him by the arm closer to the back of the room and spoke quietly. "I met him on one of my Marilyn gigs a couple of days ago."

"Oh, boy. Did he come on to you after your little strip-tease act?"

"No. Nothing like that. Hart saved me from the scumbag manager who made a pass at me. Hart is quite gallant; a true Southern gentleman."

Ethan's face softened. "Kind of like that Prince Charming sticker I saw on his shirt, huh? As long as he's good to you, that's all that matters. You deserve a good guy, Gia. What a great surprise walking in on you sucking his face."

"Ethan!" She giggled. She watched him pull out a chair and take his regular shoes off to put on his tap shoes.

"Has he got any friends?"

Gia laughed. "I don't know. I guess I could ask."

"Cool. You got a check for me?"

His question caught her off guard making her pause. "I'll have it this weekend, I promise."

He leaned his forearms on his thighs and looked up at her. "You sure? If it's gonna cause any financial strain, I can wait a little longer." His brow furrowed with concern.

She loved Ethan. Over the years, their friendship had blossomed into something truly special. He was the brother she never had, always there for her through thick and thin. She had never lied to him until recently, too embarrassed to tell him she had resorted to living in the studio because of her financial burdens. She didn't want to fail him. She couldn't. Even though she had no idea how she was going to come up with the money to pay him, she knew she'd find a way. Franko's proposition flashed through her mind. She quickly shook it off. "Absolutely, Ethan. I'll have your check this weekend."

GEORGIA ON MY MIND

CHAPTER TWELVE

The sun shone brightly through the blossoming trees in the tiny, run-down park near the studio, throwing dappled light across Gia's face. Hart wanted to put his arm around her but settled on walking closely next to her. She was draped in a giant wrap covering her so-called uniform and had changed into flats. Litter dotted the ground of the park, and a homeless man appeared to be sleeping on the top of a dilapidated picnic table. The sad scene held more tangible evidence that the area was run-down and forgotten.

"I used to play here when I was a little girl," Gia said. "It was a lot different back then. No trash. No broken playground equipment."

He looked around, trying to imagine the park during better times. "This is sad."

"Yes, it is. But there's still beauty in the rubble. I come over here sometimes when I'm in-between classes, especially on a day like today. Don't you just love springtime in Atlanta? The colors and the light…it's breathtaking."

As the bees and butterflies flew around the blooming trees and azalea bushes, Hart thought to himself that Gia was breathtaking. When she looked at him with those big blue eyes, he found himself lost in her beauty. The way her lithe body moved, even on a walk through the park, she was gorgeous, and he was falling for her.

"Stop for a second. You have something in your hair."

"Oh?"

Hart gently pulled a fuchsia redbud out of her black hair and handed it to her. "It's raining flowers."

Her smile made him bite his lip.

"So pretty." She twirled the tiny bud between her fingers as they continued down the worn path, the sounds of nearby traffic whizzing by.

They talked about everything. How she and Ethan met when they were in junior high school. The names of her littlest students she had just taught and how precocious they were. How she became fascinated with ballet after seeing *The Nutcracker* at the Fox Theater when she was five. Having Gia finally open up to him engrossed Hart. One thing they didn't talk much about was her family. When he would ask, she kept reiterating that her two closest friends, Ethan and Angel were her family. He couldn't help but wonder what her parents must have been like when she was growing up.

"What about you, Hart?"

"What about me?"

She looped her arm through his. "How did you end up in the real estate business?"

He shrugged. "That's easy. My father. He was very successful in the business and often let me tag along when I was just a kid. I loved it—the buildings, the construction crews, the tenants. I couldn't wait to wear a three-piece suit like my dad and carry a briefcase. When I was eight, I dressed like him for Halloween. I even borrowed one of his old briefcases to put my candy in."

Gia laughed. He couldn't help but join in, thinking back to a very innocent time in his life; a time when he adored his father and wanted to be just like him; a time when his dad loved him unconditionally.

"You know, this area used to be part of his territory back in the day."

"Really? I'll bet it was a lot different."

"Yes, it was. I remember coming to your strip mall. I think we may have eaten in the diner too, at some point."

Gia stopped in her tracks. "That's amazing! What are the chances of that?"

"I know."

Their time together was almost up as Gia had another class to teach at five. They strolled back through the park toward the studio. Waiting at the crosswalk for the light to turn, Hart laced his fingers with hers.

"Can I see you tonight?"

She squinted in the sunlight and looked up at him. "I'm sorry, Hart. I have a gig up in Alpharetta."

Disappointed, he tried again. "How about tomorrow night then?" He watched her cheeks blush, and she squeezed his hand. He wasn't one to give up that easily.

"I'm free on Sunday. All day, in fact. Can you wait till then?"

Sunday was several days away. "You're either crazy busy with work, or you've got a secret boyfriend hiding in your closet."

She laughed. He adored her laugh.

"I'm just busy, Hart. No boyfriend. I'm sorry."

"Don't be sorry. It's admirable. You're a hard-working twenty-first century woman. I get it. I just wish we had more quality time together. I'm enjoying getting to know you."

"Me too."

***

The rest of the week was uneventful, Gia working at all hours of the day trying to scrape together the money to pay Ethan and her other instructor, Donna. The checks from her students helped. So did the extra gigs at night. But it was still never enough. When her car was dead on

Saturday morning, she freaked out, adding more angst to her work week. One of the cooks at the diner worked part-time as a mechanic at a repair shop, and Angel sent him across the lot to take a look at her car. He determined the battery needed replacing, which in the grand scheme of things was only a minor situation. Still, she didn't need to be spending over a hundred dollars on it, not now.

Sitting at the counter of the diner, aimlessly stirring her cup of lukewarm coffee with a spoon, she stared off into space with her chin propped on her hand. Franko's proposition was tucked away in the back of her mind, but she had come up with a solution without having to stoop to his level. It was something she had promised she would never do.

"Why are you so melancholy?" Angel interrupted.

Gia sighed. "I'm not. It's nothing."

"Nothing, my foot! What's going on?" Angel crossed her arms and stared her down.

Rolling her eyes, she sat erect on the swivel seat and held her head high. "I had to pawn Aunt Caroline's ring…"

"*No!*" Angel looked like she was about to cry.

"Just hear me out, okay? It's temporary. Like a loan. I met with the pawn shop owner, and he's going to keep it in the back safe so no one will buy it. He's giving me a month to pay it off so I can get it back. It was the only way I could get ahead of these bills, Angel. That, or stripping at Franko's club."

"Girl…." The expression on Angel's face conveyed alarm. "Please don't ever do that."

"Don't worry. I won't." She mustered a tiny smile. "A minor setback. That's all this is. I'll get through it."

Angel grabbed her hand on the counter and squeezed. "We'll get through it together."

Walking back to the studio, Gia thought about the ring her aunt had left her. It was ancient and extremely valuable; an heirloom from her ancestors. She didn't fill the pawn shop owner in on the details of the exquisite stones of the piece, feeling he might take advantage of the situation if he honestly knew how valuable the jewelry was. Because they were both business owners in the area and his daughter had taken a few classes back in the day when her aunt ran the studio, he agreed to their little arrangement, promising he would hold on to the ring for thirty days.

Thirty days.

Shaking her head, she unlocked the door and sighed. At least she was caught up on her rent and had paid Ethan and Donna what she owed them in full, which bought her more time to figure out her next steps. And she had a couple of students bring friends to class, which resulted in a few extra dollars. Exhausted, she still had two gigs to go to that night. Saturdays were always the hardest, the endless hours of teaching and performing zapping her energy. She was eager to get the day over with, anticipating spending an entire Sunday with Hart.

Looking through a box of CD's that sat on the floor next to the stereo, she found what she was looking for and grinned. She turned the system on and loaded the disc, upping the volume so she could hear the music while she got ready. The sumptuous voice of Sade filled the space as she sang about love being stronger than pride. Gia's mood lightened immediately. There was something about the power of music that had a natural calming effect on her. That and art, good food, a beautiful sky, and dancing, of course. She didn't want to dwell on handing over her priceless ring to a stranger or allow the feeling of hopelessness to consume her. No. She tried to concentrate on the good that was happening in her life. The close relationships she was lucky to have, and the new ones she was creating.

Hart called her every day to check in. If she couldn't answer her phone, he always left a message. He was sweet and charming and she was smitten. The plans he was making for their day together were secretive, and he wouldn't indulge her with the details. She told him she usually rested on Sundays and might be a bit tired, to which he said not to worry; he'd make sure she was relaxed and pampered after the long, hard week.

Staring at her reflection in the small bathroom mirror, Gia carefully used her sharpened black eyeliner pencil to make a perfect beauty mark on her left cheek, her transformation into Marilyn complete. She dabbed her crimson lips with a tissue one last time before gathering the stage makeup and putting it into a small bag she loaded into her purse. The sensual beat of *No Ordinary Love* echoed throughout the space as she made her way back to the stereo to turn it off before heading out. Pausing in the middle of the floor, she couldn't help but start an impromptu dance, running her hands down her hips, the music taking over her body. Moving and bending to the rhythm of the song, the skirt of her costume twirled beautifully, her long legs and arms kicking and reaching out with precision. The freedom of dance was liberating, the song pulsating through her entire being. When it ended, she looked at herself in the wall of mirrors, her chest rising and falling. Tucking a blonde lock of wig hair back into place, she sighed happily, thankful for the impromptu release before she forged ahead into the night.

CHAPTER THIRTEEN

Hart was up earlier than usual, getting ready for his day with Gia. Thankful that the sun was out, he did a quick run through the empty park before stopping by the local market to pick up some last-minute items on his list. Only a few shoppers were in the small store that was within walking distance of the condo, allowing him to streamline his errand with efficiency. An elderly cashier offered him a smile as she rang up his purchases.

"Looks like a lovely morning for you and someone special," she said, surprising him. Was it that obvious?

Cocking his head with chagrin, he ran his hand through his sweaty hair. The conveyor belt held an assortment of items that could be deemed as romantic—expensive cheeses and fancy crackers, plump green grapes and a pint of strawberries, a box of chocolates and a giant, fresh bouquet of gorgeous red roses all insinuating a romantic rendezvous. What the cashier didn't know was he had already been to the store the previous day three separate times for special brunch and dinner ingredients.

"Uhh, yes. A few last-minute items before company arrives." He pulled out a credit card from the small pocket of his running shorts. "How much do I owe you?"

Gia was due to arrive around ten that morning. Traffic would be minimal due to the large churches in his neighborhood holding services during that time. Surveying the condo once more, he went to the arrangement of red roses he had placed on his sister's dining room table that looked peculiarly pretentious. He grabbed the clear vase and set it on the sideboard instead, opting for a single pillar candle to grace the center of the table. Satisfied, the aroma of quiche baking in the oven filtered into the room, making his stomach growl.

After a quick shower, he set the food out buffet style and glanced at his watch. In ten minutes the blue-eyed beauty would be there. Pulling out a large pitcher of fresh-squeezed orange juice, he quickly prepared two mimosas, pouring a generous dose of expensive champagne and juice into crystal flutes. As the top of the glasses fizzed with fancy bubbles, the doorbell rang. He carefully grabbed one of the flutes and trotted to the door. When he opened it, Gia was standing on the stoop with a shy smile on her face, looking like a million bucks.

"Good morning!" He smiled and offered her the drink.

Her face lit up in the morning light. "Good morning, Hart. Wow. For me?"

"Yes. Please come in." He ushered her inside, excited she had finally arrived. He had told her they'd be hanging out at his place for the day and to dress casually. She had followed his instructions and dressed in loose, drawstring pants and an oversized, soft sweater that hung sexily off one shoulder. The girl didn't have a clue how absurdly and naturally beautiful she was.

She stopped in the foyer, taking a sip of the mimosa. "Mmmm! What a great way to start my only day off."

"I was hoping you might like champagne and orange juice."

"Who doesn't?" Inhaling deeply, she looked around. "And what is that unbelievable smell coming from your kitchen?"

He watched her walk into the small space and investigate her surroundings. The quiche was still steaming, looking like he had just pulled it out of the oven from where it sat on the buffet Hart had set up. He had cut up the expensive cheese and placed it on a platter along with the crackers and grapes. She looked up at him with flushed cheeks. "You made brunch?"

"I did."

She placed her flute on the counter before wrapping her arms around his waist and hugging him tightly. "Thank you," she said softly. Yep, he had just scored. Even though the quiche wasn't homemade and bought ready-made from the store, at that moment, he was thankful for his Southern mother and sister for teaching him the ways to a woman's heart.

"I hope you're hungry," he replied, gripping her body. The long wait was over, and she was finally in his arms.

She rested her chin on his chest and looked up at him with big blue eyes. "Starving."

"Well, let's get you some sustenance for our day ahead."

The two of them sat on his sister's quaint back porch that overlooked a wooded area of the condo complex. Small, green buds dotted the tips of the oak and elm trees while the dogwood branches clung tightly to white and pink flowers. Hart had topped-off their drinks, and the two of them were animated and ravenous while eating the delicious meal. It thrilled him to watch Gia go back inside for a second helping, and when they were both finished, he cleared the small table and brought out the pitcher of juice and the bottle of champagne.

"Might as well finish this," he said, refilling her flute.

"Hart, this was divine. Thank you so much for going to all the trouble."

"No trouble at all, Gia. It's my pleasure."

Relaxed and at ease, she lay her dark head back on the seat while staring out at the scenery. A lazy smile blossomed across her face as she fingered the top of her glass. "It must be nice to live in this area. It's so peaceful and calm."

Hart rested an ankle on his knee. "It's very nice. I'm lucky to have a sister who took me in when I needed help." He took a big gulp of his drink, trying to muster the courage to ask her a few questions, her birth name at the forefront of his mind. "Gia?"

"Hmm?" she purred.

"Is your name short for 'Georgia'?"

The smile on her face faded, and she tensed. "Why would you ask me that?" she asked softly, avoiding his eyes.

Hart shifted in his seat, leaning toward her. "I met your landlord, Ed Smith, the same day I stopped by your studio. When I told him I was a friend of yours, he called you, 'Georgia.' When I asked him about it, he said it was your birth name. No big deal. I was just curious."

He observed Gia deeply inhale before she sat up perfectly straight, gripping her hands in her lap. She waited half a minute before she spoke but still wouldn't look him in the eye.

"Yes, Georgia is my birth name, but I go by Gia now. It's a long, long story, Hart. One that I really don't want to get into with you."

His face fell, and he felt like he had just ruined their perfect morning together. "I'm sorry, Gia. I didn't mean to pry. I'm just so damned attracted and interested in you... I want to get to know the real you. That's all."

Her head jerked, and she looked at him with narrow eyes. "The real me? That's what you want to know?"

"Well, yeah..."

She shook her head and stared off into the distance. "There was no 'real me' until my Aunt Caroline took me in. That's when I changed my name to 'Gia.' That's when my life really started."

Hart knew he was getting close to something, the salesman in him wanting to coerce her into telling him more—he couldn't help himself. "Well, what happened before the name change?'"

He watched her chug the sunny liquid in her glass and wipe her pink lips with the back of her hand. Her blue eyes appeared darker. "Hart, you really have no idea what you're asking me. I had a pretty traumatic childhood, and as I said before, it's something I don't care to re-live by telling you all about it."

Standing, he knew he had crossed a line and held his hand out in a truce, trying to salvage their time together. Gia hesitated before allowing him to pull her up out of the chair and into his sturdy arms. He could feel her shaking.

"You're trembling." Running his hand down the back of her hair, he gripped her tighter. "I'm so sorry, Gia. I won't bring it up again." He could feel her nod into his chest.

They continued to embrace, neither one of them saying a word. He kissed her temple and leaned his forehead on the top of her head, silently chastising himself for ruining the morning. Her soft lips grazed his cheek, peppering his skin with subtle kisses, surprising him. Pulling back, he looked into her eyes, cupping her face gently with his hands. The first kiss he offered was on her forehead, then her eyes, cheeks, nose and finally, her mouth. Her hands fisted in his shirt as she opened up to him, their tongues, tentative at first before passion consumed them.

Hart couldn't hold back. His hands slid down her curves and gripped her buttocks. Gia's kisses were like gasoline on his fire, igniting something primal from within.

"Take me to your bedroom," she whispered breathily into his ear. He couldn't speak, grasping her hand and leading her quickly through the house, up the stairs and into the spare bedroom that had become his home for almost a year. He stood within inches of the bed and watched her close the door behind them. Her blue eyes had life in them again; her eyebrow arched provocatively as she moved toward him like a jungle cat. Her short, dark hair was tousled from their make-out session, and her sweater hung dramatically off one shoulder, dangerously close to revealing her bare breast. There was no way she was wearing a bra under that thing.

She jerked at his pants, making him inhale sharply, his bulging boner apparent. With his pants around his ankles, he was at her mercy as he stood there in his boxers. She lifted the edges of his t-shirt and swiftly brought it up and over his head before freeing herself from her sweater. He was right—she was braless underneath. He reached out to touch her full breasts, her hand immediately grabbing at his wrist.

"No. Not yet," she whispered lustfully. He nodded and let her lead the way. As she slowly eased herself down to the floor onto her knees, she took his boxers down with her. When her soft hands finally touched his sensitive hardness, he shivered with want. She looked up at him and smiled before leaning forward with her mouth wide open. As her lips came down on his skin, he held his breath. Closing his eyes, he ran his hand over her head and pulsed to the slow rhythm of her mouth sucking his penis. She used her tongue to run his length and sucked on his balls, causing him to see stars.

"Do you like that?" He heard her ask.

"Oh, god, yes. You're incredible."

Her mouth consumed him, and she gripped him harder, twirling her wet tongue around his shaft. He fisted his hands in her hair, pushing deeper into her mouth, aware that he was about to come undone.

"Gia... I can't...I can't hold back much longer." She nodded, sucking him even harder. "*Gia*!"

Releasing himself from her mouth, she took hold of him and jerked him off until he came all over her bare chest. He swayed backward and sat unexpectedly on the bed, the aftershocks of the sexual encounter pulsating through his body. He tried to get a hold of his breathing as he took in the image of Gia biting her lip, her chest glistening in the daylight with his manhood. Grabbing his t-shirt, he ran it across her breasts.

"I'm sorry about that. I made a mess."

Not saying a word, she watched him intently, her nipples erect as he cleaned her off. When he finished, he tossed the shirt across the room where it landed on the floor near a chair. "Stand up for me," he requested.

When she was standing, he ran his hands up and down her exposed skin before slowly untying the drawstring of her pants. They fell to the ground, and she stepped out of them. The fabric of her panties curled in on itself as he tugged and pulled them off. She stepped out of those too.

Looking up at her with wide eyes, he ran his fingers across her soft mound. "You're so fucking beautiful," he managed to utter. He continued, dipping his finger into her wetness, causing her to moan. "Oh, yes." Gripping his shoulders, she looked down at him moving to the rhythm of his hand.

"I want to make love to you, Gia. I have protection in the nightstand."

Not a word was said as she pushed him down on the bed and straddled him. Chuckling, he shook his head. "You may be in charge at the dance studio, but right now, I want to drive this train." Grasping her shoulders, he quickly flipped her over to where he was straddling her. Stretching his arm, he reached for the nightstand, opened the drawer, and pulled out a silver packet, his growing bulge throbbing between his thighs.

"You want me, Gia?" he asked, his breath quickening.

She nodded beneath him. He leaned down and skirted his lips across her cheek, leaning into her ear. "I wanna hear you say it."

She swallowed hard before he heard her sweet voice. "Please, I need you now."

Quickly, he ripped at the foil packet and fumbled to get the condom on his engorged manhood. Gia helped, gently holding him in place. Their eyes locked in on each other as Hart eased himself into her wet folds. She gasped, arching her back, the tightness sending a jolt of pure pleasure through his body. Wrapping her strong legs around his waist, they moved together in a steady rhythm, climbing faster and faster. It had been a long, long time since he had been with a woman, even longer since he had been with someone so utterly perfect for him. Gripping her gorgeous body in his arms, he shuddered in delicious pain as his orgasm hit him head on, and for a moment, ecstasy consumed him.

CHAPTER FOURTEEN

Gia lay sprawled across his naked body, fast asleep, with the midday sun shining brightly into the bedroom in large slanted beams at the foot of the bed. Small particles of dust floated in the brightness, and the warmth of the sun penetrated his bare feet in the path of light. His arms were around her, and he lightly ran his index finger across her bangs, wholly satiated from their first time making love. Her graceful, athletic curves were intoxicating, and she moved smoothly like a river, the power underneath sweeping him away in her current. It was everything he could have imagined, and more.

Letting her sleep, he thought about their conversation on the back porch and was troubled. She had told him her childhood was traumatic but gave no details. Not wanting to upset her, he stopped himself from asking too many questions, having no idea what she had been through. If they were going to continue their love affair, he would have to coerce the information from her somehow gently.

His own childhood was idyllic, having grown up in a country club neighborhood with an all-American family who truly loved him. His parents had been married for almost thirty-five years, a noble feat in this day and age.

The only trauma he ever experienced was disappointing his father from time to time when he was involved in minor fist fights at school or punching holes in his bedroom wall out of teenage angst. He took after his grandfather who had an angry streak that would rear its ugly head quickly, and then disappear as if nothing had happened. His sister Katie was the sensitive sibling in the family, having to endure his hormonal outbursts while growing up together in the same household. Before she left on tour with her country music boyfriend, she had commented how proud she was that he had finally grown up and was taking responsibility for his actions without angrily damaging property or people.

Hart looked down at Gia's sleeping face, her dark eyelashes curling upward like soft feathers. He could feel an ember of something strong brewing in his chest. Gone was the rage of his past. What he felt now was tender and caring. He pulled her closer, realizing he felt the need to protect her, to look after her. From what, he wasn't sure.

Gia stirred in his embrace, her eyes fluttering open. His heart skipped a beat as he took in the captivating, endless blue of her eyes.

"Hi," she said sleepily.

"Hi," he replied. "You looked so peaceful sleeping in my arms. Do you feel better?"

She inhaled deeply, a smile of satisfaction blossoming across her face. "Mmmhumm. I was out cold."

He watched her sit up and stretch, reaching her long arms up into the air. He stifled a grin as he noticed her hair sticking straight up in the back, making her appear very young. Her shoulders lazily slumped as she looked back at him, her dark nipples on her bare chest a stark contrast to her milky-white skin.

"What time is it? Did I waste the whole afternoon sleeping?"

Hart sat up and ran his hand over the back of her hair gently before pulling her forward to kiss her mouth. "No.

We've got all day and night."

"Yay," she replied, rubbing the tip of her nose with his. He chuckled.

"Why don't you take a long soak in my sister's garden tub while I take care of a few things? You need to continue to relax on your only day off."

Her eyes lit up. "A garden tub? Are you sure she wouldn't mind?"

"Nope. She's on tour with her country music boyfriend somewhere in the northwest. Her tub is deep and optimal for relaxing. I insist."

She smiled with pleasure as if tempted by the invitation to soak in a deep tub. "Well, if you insist…"

*

Gia pointed her long leg up into the air and ran the loofah sponge down her skin, causing tiny bubbles to skate and skim across the top of the water. To be immersed in the decadent warmth was heaven. She couldn't even remember the last time she had soaked in a tub this big. Leisurely washing her hair was another indulgence, and she took her sweet time, enjoying the simple task she had taken for granted. Lying back with her head propped up on a soft towel, she lightly traced the top of the bath water and stared out the un-obscured window highlighting the corner tub that overlooked the wooded lot below. The view was magnificent with budding trees under the blue sky dotted with white clouds. She had finally relaxed, thanks to Hartford Parker and his generous insistence on doting on her hand and foot.

The door cracked open, and he peeked his head in. "May I come in?"

Gia turned her wet head and smiled broadly. "Of course."

She watched him enter, his sweatpants hanging off his sexy hips and his full lips looking oh-so-tempting. Grabbing a towel, he placed it on the side of the tub before sitting, his eyes taking in her naked body under the water.

"Good. You look relaxed. And clean."

She giggled, allowing him to take her all in. "This has been pure heaven."

"You don't have a bathtub at your place?"

Her eyebrows shot up. "No. I…I wish I did."

He nodded. "Well, I'm glad you could enjoy this. Do you need any help with anything? I'm your personal cabana boy today. At your beck and call." He grinned, tilting his head playfully.

"Wow! My very own cabana boy? I guess you could help me out of the tub?"

"I would love to." He stood and yanked the towel he had been sitting on, fluffing it open. Extending his arm, Gia put her hand in his, allowing him to pull her up and out of the tepid water, and he immediately wrapped her up. Water dripped from her face as she looked up at him, cocooned in his arms.

"Aren't you going to dry me off?" she asked softly.

His lips curled up to one side as he pulled the towel off and gently started to dry her. She clasped her hands in front of her chest, watching him bend low and start at her feet, slowly moving his way up. The friction of the fabric against her soft mound caused her to inhale sharply, and he paused to pay particular attention to that area. Bringing the towel up to her chest, she unclasped her hands and allowed him to dry her tummy and breasts, aware of the tingling happening between her thighs again.

"Turn around so I can get your back," he whispered.

Turning, she grasped the vanity and watched his reflection behind her as he continued drying her back and shoulders. He flipped the towel over her head and massaged the top of her head, drying her hair. When he pulled it off, she laughed at her reflection in the mirror, her hair sticking out in all directions. Suddenly, his lips were on her neck, and she rolled her head to the side. His hands came up to her middle and squeezed her breasts. She could feel his hardness pressing against her bottom.

"Did I do a good job drying you off?" he whispered seductively.

"Oh, yes."

His hands made a trail down to her clit, his fingers eagerly teasing the swollen nub. "Mmm. I prefer you nice and wet," he uttered.

Gia was lost in the sensation, panting with want, her eyes rolling into the back of her head. She was flying high as he expertly stroked her, on the cusp of another orgasm. Gripping the vanity, she pulsed with his hand, his body heavy against her back, feeling like she was about to explode. What was it about mirrors and this man? To see herself come undone in the reflection was sexy and hot!

"That's it," he encouraged, his staccato breath warm in her ear.

Her toes curled, and she bit her lower lip so she wouldn't cry out, her insides shattering with a warm surge. With her eyes tightly shut, she slowly came down from the intense desire and leaned heavily against his rock-hard body. He kissed her cheek several times, allowing her to come back to life after the experience. When she opened her eyes, his reflection greeted her with a knowing smile. Heat rushed up the back of her neck and settled into her cheeks.

"I'm glad I could be of service," he teased.

She turned around and rewarded him with a long passionate kiss.

They watched a movie during the afternoon, lounging on the L-shaped couch and eating microwave popcorn and dollar candy Hart had picked up at the store. Gia was nestled against him, popping Jr. Mints into her mouth, enjoying his companionship and laughter during the romantic comedy she had picked out on cable. It was as if they had been a couple for longer than a week, their chemistry and his easy-going nature unexpected and welcome. At one point in the afternoon, he had her shift and put her feet in his lap where he proceeded to give her the best foot massage of her entire life. Being a dancer, she coveted foot massages; the long hours on her feet and endless beating they took often causing soreness and fatigue. The way his strong hands kneaded and his thumbs dug into her pressure points almost caused her to have another full-blown orgasm right there on the couch.

When it came time for dinner, they stood side-by-side in the galley kitchen and made homemade pizza, placing a variety of toppings all over a pre-made crust. The laughter continued, and they flirted while sipping on bottled beer and listening to classic rock cranked on the stereo. The light of a single pillar candle in the middle of the dining room table cast a sexy glow across Hart's face as he poured her a glass of red wine, the music changed to soft jazz. He hadn't questioned her any more about her past or her family. She almost felt guilty for being thoroughly pampered while withholding information from him. He was a good guy, only trying to get to know her better.

Pushing her empty plate away, she took another sip of wine and sighed, enjoying the candlelight dancing in his brown eyes.

"Did you get enough to eat?" he asked quietly while the melody of *My Funny Valentine* echoed out of a lone, sexy saxophone.

"I did. It's been the best day. Thanks for going to all the trouble."

Shaking his head, he poured the remnants of the wine bottle into her glass. "No trouble at all. And you're right. It has been the best day."

She clasped her hands on her lap underneath the table. "I want to apologize to you, Hart."

A flash of concern swept over his face. "Apologize for what?"

"For not being forthcoming with you this morning. You asked me some normal questions any guy would ask a girl he's trying to get to know, and I shut you down. That wasn't fair."

"Gia, it's okay. You obviously don't want to talk about it, so I'm not going to push."

"But I do want to talk about it now. You deserve to know the truth. It's just…hard. But I'm willing to try."

Hart reached his hand up and stroked her cheek. "Sweetheart, you don't have to tell me anything. I'm the one who's sorry for badgering you like a dumbass. It's all good."

Gia bit her lower lip and nodded, staring down at her plate. Without looking at him, she spoke very quietly. "I never knew who my father was." Letting those awful words hang in the air, she nervously twisted the napkin in her lap before forging ahead. "My mother was an exotic dancer for an Atlanta club, which led to a horrible drug habit. She died of an overdose when I was nine." When she mustered the strength to look him in the eye after finally divulging her secrets, she immediately noticed his expression was one of sympathy and concern.

"Oh, Gia…"

"No, it's okay. It was tough growing up without real parents like most people had, but I'm at peace with it all now. You need to know that. I really like you, and I want to continue to see you. I don't want there to be anything weird between us."

"Come here," he requested.

She went to him and sat in his lap. He laced his fingers with hers and looked at her with intensity. "I'm proud of you for having the courage to share that with me. It means a lot. You can tell me more if you want, or leave it where it is. Whatever you're comfortable with. I want to continue to see you too. You've done a real number on me."

They sat in silence for several seconds before he kissed the tips of her fingers and chuckled. "I don't think I've ever eaten quiche with a woman before."

His random comment made her laugh out loud, her heart surging with affection. She had finally met a man she could confide in—a man who truly made her feel safe and adored. Grabbing his face by the cheeks, she pulled him in for a passionate, wine-soaked kiss as the sexy jazz floated all around them.

CHAPTER FIFTEEN

Sitting tall with his briefcase perched on his lap, Hart waited patiently in the lobby area of a massive office building in downtown Atlanta. He had finally secured a job interview with one of the top real estate firms in the country after months of emails and networking events. As always, he had thoroughly done his homework, researching the man at the helm of the firm, Stephen Kaufman. He was a native Atlanta man himself and a fellow graduate of the University of Georgia. What thrilled him the most was knowing Mr. Kaufman's wife, Jessica Southers graduated in the same high school class with his sister, Katie, ten years ago. Perhaps, they had known each other. This was a good sign.

"Mr. Kaufman will see you now." The polite receptionist escorted him to the large wooden doors that opened up to a narrow hallway. "It's the last door on the left."

"Thank you." Hart straightened his tie and strode confidently down the pristine hall. There was no way he was going to fuck this up. He firmly knocked on the door and heard a booming baritone voice telling him to come in. A tall, distinguished-looking man with salt and pepper hair greeted him.

"Hartford Parker."

"Mr. Kaufman. It's a pleasure." The two men shook hands.

"The pleasure is mine. And please, call me Stephen." He motioned with his hand to an empty wingback chair near a wall of windows overlooking the Atlanta skyline. "Hartford. Cool name. Can I call you Hart?"

"Absolutely."

"Great! I've been looking at your portfolio for quite some time. You come highly recommended by several of our colleagues in the business. I'm surprised you haven't been snatched up since you've been back from…where was it? Washington?" Stephen sat behind a large desk thumbing through a folder. The entire office space was immaculate.

"Yes, sir. DC. I've been back for almost six months."

"Why the long hiatus? Biding your time for the best offer?"

Hart shifted uncomfortably in the stiff chair. Mr. Kaufman had to have heard about his indiscretion. Not sure how to approach the subject he replied, "I guess you could say that."

Stephen laughed before looking at him knowingly. "Yeah, I know all about what happened in DC."

"You do?"

"Of course. I have to say it was pretty incredible what you tried to pull off behind closed doors in the executive office. And at a party, no less." His smile was almost a sneer.

Hart's stomach dropped to his knees. How dare this big shot Atlanta broker taunt him. Did he think he was better than him? His face flushed with embarrassment as he stood to leave. "I'm sorry for wasting your time—"

Stephen interrupted him. "No, wait! I didn't mean it like that. Sit. Please."

Hart looked at him with narrow eyes, not sure if he

should sit or run.

"Please." The tone of his voice was insistent.

He slowly slunk down into the chair, his confidence already out the door.

"You know my wife, Jessica and your sister graduated in the same class in high school. What are the chances of that?"

"Yeah, I know."

"Jess remembers you well. You were a couple of years ahead of them, but you certainly made an impression on her. She remembers you being a very popular, strong athlete."

Hart sighed. "I don't know about that. I played football and had some good friends. Nothing out of the ordinary for high school."

Stephen nodded. "Yeah, I know your type. You're a good-looking, successful guy, Hart. I'll bet you've had more than one beautiful girl tempt you during your career. I look at it as a positive attribute. Let's just say, I've had my fair share as well if you know what I mean." His eyebrow raised significantly. "We're a lot alike, you and me."

They were suddenly interrupted by a cell phone ringing. Stephen looked down before abruptly getting up. "Sorry, Hart. I gotta take this call from the West Coast. I'll only be a minute." He excused himself and stepped into the hall.

Hart wasn't sure if he liked where their conversation was headed and was thankful for the reprieve. His buddy, Mitch Montgomery, had warned him that Stephen Kaufman was a very successful but shrewd businessman. He obviously didn't know the dude was a hound dog as well. Standing, he did his best to feign disinterest in the call and noticed several industry awards adorning the rich mahogany bookcases. Each faceted trophy seemed perfectly positioned to cast prisms of light, drawing the eyes of visitors, flaunting the success of the firm. He also saw a family portrait of Stephen with his beautiful wife,

Jessica and their four, tiny, blonde-headed daughters all dressed in matching pink outfits. They looked like the perfect all-American family. His stomach turned, knowing the guy had probably cheated on his wife and kids with the way he had been talking earlier. He wasn't like this guy. Not anymore.

Stephen came back in, startling Hart. "Sorry about that. Where were we?"

For the next thirty minutes, the two men talked about the current Atlanta real estate market, Stephen steering clear from their earlier conversation about what happened in DC. The focus was on the impressive multi-million-dollar portfolio Hart had secured for his last firm and what he might be able to bring to the table. The man was more than knowledgeable, and Hart hated to admit, he was impressed. To work for Kaufman and Associates would be a big step back into the corporate world of real-estate, even if the guy was a cheater. In a bold move that surprised even himself, he readily accepted a lucrative offer right there on the spot, thoughts of their earlier conversation about indiscretions tucked away in the back of his mind.

"Thanks so much Stephen. I won't let you down." He vigorously shook his hand, relieved that he was finally back in business.

"Happy to have you onboard, Hart. I have a good feeling about you. You're going to be a great asset to our team. We'll get your office set up the first of next week. Welcome to Kaufman and Associates."

***

"You start next week?" Gia was flabbergasted Hart had accepted a job on the spot, and on his very first interview in Atlanta.

"Yep. I'm back in the game!" He leaned forward and kissed her quickly on the lips. "We're gonna need to celebrate this weekend. Please tell me you have Friday or Saturday night off."

She shook her head in disappointment. "I have Sunday off. That's it."

Hart nodded, offering an accepting smile. "Then Sunday it is." He kissed her again. "Sorry I interrupted your class. I just wanted to tell you the good news."

They were standing in the parking lot, Gia in her ballet slippers and leotard, Hart in his expensive business suit. The late afternoon was overcast, the wind blowing colorful flowers off the blooming trees, scattering them like confetti at a ticker-tape parade.

"I'm glad you came by. Ethan was more than happy to take over for a few minutes." She leaned into his touch as he brushed her hair from her cheek. "I'm so proud of you, Hart. You deserve a break."

"So do you." He pulled her in for a lingering hug. "I wish I could take you to my place and celebrate right now."

She giggled into his lapels. "Me too. I'll text you later before I head to my gig tonight."

"Where is it this time?" He always seemed genuinely interested in what she was doing and where she was going.

"It's another bachelor party. All of the springtime weddings in Atlanta this time of year are keeping me pretty busy."

"I'll say. I'll be glad when things slow down, and I can have you all to myself in the evenings." He squeezed her tightly. "If things end early and you're not too tired, I could always come to your place tonight. I've been dying to see where you live finally."

His comment took her by surprise. He still didn't know she was technically homeless, living in the closet in her studio. Over the past few weeks, she had somehow managed to divert his attention away from the subject, coming up with creative excuses to keep his curiosity at bay. She couldn't possibly tell him now. Focused on saving every penny so she could pay bills and get her aunt's ring back, Gia was working her ass off, day and night. She just needed a little more time.

"Ummm, yeah. I'll let you know if things end early."

"Good."

Keeping secrets had always been easy for the little girl once known as Georgia Bates. Growing up with a stripper for a mother, she was often left alone during the night; used to taking care of herself, relying on no one. When her mother took a turn for the worse and started abusing more drugs and alcohol, Georgia did her best to take care of her in their tiny, dilapidated apartment located in a run-down neighborhood. Her only solace was escaping to her aunt's dance studio two miles away. She was a scrappy little girl who did well in school and learned at an early age how to cook and clean so she could survive.

Even though her Aunt Caroline was estranged from Georgia's mother, she encouraged her niece to dance, taking the little girl under her wing and grooming her to be a prima ballerina. She covered the cost of everything from ballet slippers and apparel to private lessons. Her aunt's involvement in her life was noble, and Gia remembered often feeling guilty for telling her aunt elaborate lies about how her mother was working steadily and making homemade meals every night when she came home. Her aunt learned later at a custody hearing that Georgia often went without meals, her mother disappearing for days on end, leaving her daughter to fend for herself in depressing conditions.

Two days before her ninth birthday, Georgia came home from school to find her mother dead on the floor of their living room with a needle still sticking out of her arm. Ruby Anne Bates, mother of little Georgia Ruth Bates, died at the age of twenty-eight on a cloudy winter day. Her only sister, Caroline was awarded full custody. The night she moved in with her aunt was the night little Georgia boldly decided to shorten her name to Gia, vowing never to look back. Gia would always feel indebted to her beloved aunt who fiercely loved and believed in her the brief time they were together. What would she think of her now? Would she be disappointed? Would she regret leaving the studio in her hands? Once again, Gia was at a crossroads. But the scrappy little girl from the wrong side of the tracks wasn't about to give up.

She watched Hart weave his Mercedes through the parking lot and pull into the afternoon traffic. It was hard for her to watch him go. She wanted so badly to go with him, to open up to him entirely. But duty called, and she had children to teach and stressful decisions to make. Unfortunately, she had lost another two students from the roster that week. The hits to her failing business kept on coming, including the recent news that her instructor, Donna, was moving to Savannah with her boyfriend. She would have to consolidate her remaining classes and sweetly ask Ethan to help with the overload. Walking back into the studio, she had to stifle a smile while watching her friend prance around the room with little girlies following him from behind. They took to him like ducks to water. A pang of guilt traveled to her heart, knowing she was keeping secrets from not just Hart, but her loyal friends as well. Ethan had always been there for her since they were kids—a true friend who she could always count on. The time was rapidly approaching, and the truth would have to be revealed, to everyone. Until then, she buried her secrets deep in her gut, resisted the desire to purge her guilt, and held onto her threadbare dreams for dear life.

GEORGIA ON MY MIND

CHAPTER SIXTEEN

This was an uncomfortable situation. Hart chugged the remnants of his whiskey and set the empty highball glass down on the mahogany bar of the upscale restaurant. He'd been working for Kaufman and Associates for a little over a month and was becoming quite familiar with the weeknight schedule of his boss, Stephen Kaufman. Trying not to be too conspicuous, he shifted in his seat and could see Stephen talking intimately with a young woman near the restrooms in the corner. He had seen this woman before at a real estate conference and a couple of lunch and dinner meetings with potential clients. At first, he thought she was a colleague in the business and didn't think anything of it. But when she showed up tonight, and he noticed the way Stephen grabbed her ass as they excused themselves so they could discuss an urgent matter, he knew.

This woman was Mr. Kaufman's mistress.

"Would you like another, sir?" the bartender asked politely.

"No thanks." He stood and rummaged in his wallet for some cash, flinging it on the bar. His revelation made his gut twist, knowing this married man—his boss was potentially on the verge of ruining the lives of his beautiful wife and four children. They didn't deserve this, he was sure of it. There was a time not too long ago when Hart wouldn't have cared either way. But he was a changed man. He had hurt people with his poor choices, including his own family, and he didn't want to ever go through that again.

Accelerating in and out of evening traffic, he thought about how he and Gia had been exclusively dating each other for almost two months. The poor girl still worked way too hard, but she always found time for him, their favorite day of the week Sunday when they would devote every second to each other. Aside from his boss having an affair, his new job was going well, his due diligence in finding funding for Mr. Ed Smith's crumbling property a priority. It was slow going, but he was determined to find a solution and help the woman he was falling in love with in the process.

His phone buzzed, his boss's number flashing on the console screen. Hart grimaced, knowing he was going to have to explain why he left the restaurant.

"Hartford Parker," he answered.

"Hart! Where did you go? I wanted you to meet someone special."

"Well, you seemed kind of busy, sir. I didn't think you'd mind if I slipped out and called it a night."

The phone muffled before Stephen came back on. "That's fine. Have a great weekend. I know I will!" The man laughed out loud. Hart shook his head, wondering if he had ever been that blatantly bad. "I'll see you bright and early on Monday."

Before Hart could respond, the phone went dead. He ran his hand through his hair while gripping the steering wheel with the other. What a low-life. Did he even care he had a wife and four young daughters waiting at home for him? What kind of excuse did he give to Jessica and their children? How many times had she endured disappointment from this guy? Hart was suddenly wondering if taking the position at Kaufman and Associates had been such a good idea after all. Of course, his job brought in great money for which he was thankful; and it got him back into the competitive real estate market. But the job also brought up uncomfortable memories of his old habits, blatantly slapping him in the face. Stephen had said he wanted him to meet someone. Was he going to introduce him to his mistress?

His console lit up again, this time with a text message from Gia.

Can you meet me at the hot light? I got off early, and I'm hungry.
Hart grinned from ear to ear.
I'll be there in ten minutes.

***

Gia could see Hart's Mercedes pull into the familiar parking lot of the Krispy Kreme from her rearview mirror. She swiped at a rouge tear that trickled down her cheek, anxious to see the man who always managed to calm her. A few minutes before, she had listened to a voicemail from the pawn shop owner, letting her know they had an interested buyer in her aunt's ring. The guy had told her he'd give her one more chance to come and claim it before it was gone forever. She was grateful for the extra time—through her convincing, the guy had already extended their deal by a couple of weeks. But she was still way behind financially and knew in the back of her mind she would probably never see the ring again.

Earlier, she had managed to slip off her Marilyn dress in the car and pull on some yoga pants and a t-shirt. On top of the sad news of her aunt's ring, her gig that night had been atrocious with lots of eager, grabbing hands from inebriated men at a bachelor party. The groom-to-be had even offered her a thousand dollars to come back to his hotel room for a "last hurrah." The thought of quick cash had her mind wander to the unimaginable fleeting idea of saying "yes," but ultimately, she couldn't wait to get out of

121

there, wanting more than anything to feel Hart surround her with his protective arms.

He parked right next to her, and she watched him get out and trot excitedly to the door, opening it quickly. "Hey, sweet thing!" he said, pulling her out of the car and embracing her in a tight squeeze.

Inhaling his familiar scent, she sighed contentedly, gripping him snugly. When she didn't let go, she could feel him tense.

"Hey… hey, what's going on? Are you okay?" He held her arms and pulled back, looking at her face with concern.

She offered him a heartfelt smile and nodded. "I'm just really happy to see you."

His countenance relaxed, and his features softened. "You have no idea how happy I am to see you too."

Meeting for donuts and coffee had become one of their favorite pastimes, talking for hours without a care in the world while consuming Hart's favorite childhood treat. Situated in their usual corner booth with hot donuts and caffeine, Hart began animatedly telling her about his boss's secret girlfriend.

"I don't know, Gia. It was weird. I felt like I was betraying his wife, Jessica, by witnessing it."

She nodded. "That's unprofessional of him to expose you to his secret life. Has he ever asked you to cover for him? Anything like that?"

"No. But I wouldn't put it past the guy. You know, he's great in business; one of the top brokers in the southeast. But I really can't stand this side of him. It makes my stomach turn. I can't help but think that's how people viewed me in DC. It's probably the only reason he hired me."

Gia reached for his hand across the table and squeezed. "Stop it. You're nothing like him, Hart. He's a married man. When you lived in DC, you were single, sowing your wild oats, celebrating a *huge* milestone."

"Still doesn't make what I did acceptable."

"At least you learned a lesson and moved on, right?" She watched him struggle to agree. "Hart, you're a one-woman-man now. At least, I hope you are." She kept her tone teasing, grateful the conversation focused on him.

He smiled as he leaned across the table to kiss her sugary lips. "You're the only one I want, Gia. You know that." Taking a quick sip of coffee, he changed the subject. "How was your night? You look tired."

She slumped against the back of the booth, her false eyelashes feeling heavy on her eyelids. "I am. Tonight was... rough."

"What do you mean? Did something happen?" He bristled.

She shook her head. "It's just these rambunctious bachelor parties. The guys sometimes assume they can offer more money to keep me from leaving." She wanted to be honest with him about her aunt's ring and tell him the truth about being tempted by the quick money, but she knew it would probably make him angry. He had warned her early on when they were first getting to know each other that he had a short fuse. Apparently, it was something he inherited from his grandfather. She had seen it surface a handful of times, usually in deplorable Atlanta traffic, but it never caused her to be concerned.

"I hate that job, Gia. I remember the very first night we met when that manager made a pass at you. I've offered before, and I'll offer again. Please, let me help you financially until you can get back on your feet. You won't have to do this anymore. To be honest, I don't *want* you to do this anymore."

Her heart fluttered with hope. Could she accept his generous offer and allow him to take care of her? She had *always* been on her own. The thought of a man being in control made her uneasy. She glanced at her half-eaten donut on the paper napkin in front of her, her appetite replaced with embarrassment. "You're getting back on your feet too, Hart. I'm making ends meet. It's just hard sometimes. It's not forever."

Hart threw his napkin down in a huff and crossed his arms. "What if I don't want you exposed to this kind of harassment anymore, huh, Gia? I worry every weekend about some strange guy groping you or attacking you after a gig. Why do you continue to subject yourself to these kinds of sleazy advances? You're so much better than that! Why do you keep going back for more? And don't say it's because of the money."

Gia met his heated gaze and nodded slightly. "But you know it is. Look on the bright side, Hart. At least I'm not an exotic dancer in a club like my mother was."

"*Damnit!*" He suddenly stood and paced with his hands on his hips. She knew right then she had pushed a hot button, his short fuse erupting in a blast of anger. Why she said that about her mother, she wasn't sure.

A few curious patrons looked their way as Gia stood slowly. "I'm sorry, Hart. I shouldn't have said that. You're very generous, but this is something I need to work out for myself, okay?" She wanted to reach out and touch him, to reassure him that her job with the Atlanta entertainment company wasn't forever.

"Yep," he managed to say through gritted teeth. "I'm not hungry anymore. I'll walk you to your car."

Disappointed, she nodded and grabbed her purse, following him. When they got to their cars, he opened her door. She paused, hoping he'd at least give her a kiss goodnight. When she realized that wasn't going to happen, she got in the driver's seat with tears welling in her eyes. "I'm sorry about tonight. It was good to see you." Her voice was tinged with sadness as she looked up at him.

"I'll see you later, Gia. Drive safely." He slammed the door and quickly got in his car, leaving her alone.

Turning the key in the ignition, Gia waited before backing out. The night had not gone as planned, and she was upset they had quarreled. It was their first official fight as a couple, her day becoming the worst in ages. His intentions were honorable, but he needed to understand that she had been on her own for most of her life and wanted to figure things out for herself. He, too, was in the middle of a transition, and she didn't want to hinder his progress. Swiping at her wet cheeks, she put the car in reverse, ready to get back to her studio and collapse after the long day.

*

Hart seethed. Why did Gia keep refusing to let him help her? Of all the women he had dated over the years, she was the most stubborn and independent, which drove him crazy. It was also why he was so drawn to her. He hated that he allowed his temper to erupt in a public place. And this was the first time his anger had been directed at her, which surprised him because they usually got along so well. Driving two car lengths behind her, he couldn't help but feel remorse for his behavior. He knew he was acting like an asshole. Gia worked too hard, and she didn't deserve him chastising her on top of everything else. He had commented on how tired she looked, and now he had ruined the evening by acting like an entitled prick. Determined to make things right, he decided to follow her home and apologize with a long, overdue kiss.

The Friday night traffic was congested, and Hart had a hard time keeping up with her. He was surprised when she turned into the strip mall of her dance studio and thought she might be going to the diner to commiserate with her friend, Angel. But she didn't go into the restaurant. She went straight into the studio.

Perplexed, he parked in the shadows and waited fifteen minutes to see if she might have forgotten something and would come back out. When she didn't, he decided to find out what was going on. Perhaps she was letting off steam and dancing in the open space. Or maybe she was working in her office to get her mind off their disagreement, which made him feel worse. Determined to make things right, he banged on the door three times.

"Gia? Gia, it's me, Hart. Open up, sweetie."

There was silence on the other end. He banged another three times.

"Gia, come on! Open up! It's Hart."

He heard the click of the deadbolt and peered through the crack in the door and could see Gia's face devoid of any makeup. She was dressed in pajamas and had slippers on her feet.

"What do you want, Hart? I'm…I'm working."

Something wasn't right. He could feel it. He pushed on the door and let himself in, looking around the room to make sure they were alone.

"There's no one here if that's what you're wondering," she said, her voice laced with irritation.

He closed the door and locked it before looking at her with wide eyes. "Why are you dressed like that?"

Her blue eyes were big, and he couldn't help but think she looked nervous. "I told you. I'm working. I got comfortable."

"Bullshit," he said tersely, walking past her to the hallway that ran between the kitchen, the bathroom, and her office. He briskly surveyed the rooms in confusion. Products including a toothbrush and facial cleaner scattered across the sink in the tiny bathroom, remnants of her red lipstick on a facecloth. After surveying the rooms a second time, he didn't see the clothes she had been wearing earlier.

"What are you doing?" she asked tentatively, keeping a healthy distance from him.

"Where are your clothes?"

"My clothes?"

"Yes, Gia. Your clothes. The ones you were wearing at Krispy Kreme. Where are they?" He couldn't help it that his tone was loud and clipped.

"Why would you ask such a weird question?"

"Are they in here?" He grabbed the handle of the storage room door and tried to turn it, but it was locked.

126

"Are your clothes in there, Gia?"

He watched her back away from him with what looked like fear in her wide blue eyes. She shook her head slowly.

"Unlock the door, Gia. I need to see."

She shook her head more vigorously. He was running out of patience.

"*Open the goddamn door, Gia!*"

She continued to stand there, her face paling. In a rage, Hart kicked the door twice before it flew open, revealing the secret she'd been keeping from him all these weeks. Holding his breath, he stumbled inside and frantically looked around. He noticed right away the clothes she had been wearing draped over a chair. A pillow and sheets were covering an old couch, and an ancient television perched on a folding table was broadcasting the eleven o'clock news with the sound muted. Everything suddenly made sense. *This* was where she lived. *This* was why they never met at her place. She didn't have a place. She was living in a storage closet.

Hart was overcome with guilt and emotion and scrambled to get out of the depressing space. Gia had left the hallway and was almost out the front door of the studio when he stopped her, slapping the door shut and pinning her against it.

"Don't go, Gia. Please…"

"*No!*" She screamed when he touched her. "You're not supposed to know… I didn't want you to know!"

He pulled her into his arms, his heart racing. "Shhh, It's okay."

They slid against the door down to the floor, and she wept in his arms. He didn't know what to say and let her cry, his own tears spilling onto his cheeks as he felt sincere remorse for not recognizing her predicament earlier in their relationship. One thing was for sure—he wasn't about to allow his girlfriend to continue to live in such conditions. Her situation was dire, and he'd been blind to it.

"You're not alone, Gia. Please, let me help you. Let me finally take care of you."

CHAPTER SEVENTEEN

They sat next to each other at the tiny kitchen table in the studio breakroom. Hart watched as she stirred sugar into hot tea, the rims of her beautiful eyes tinged with red.

"You've been living here for how long?" he asked tenderly.

"Several months," she replied in a whisper.

He had somehow managed to get her to calm down and agree to tell him everything.

"Where do you bathe, Gia? There isn't a bathtub or a shower in this space."

She wrapped her hands around the chipped mug and sighed. "There's a drain in the bathroom. I usually just stand over it and use a sponge from the sink. It's not that bad."

It was worse than he thought.

"You don't even have a stove or an oven, just that tiny refrigerator and microwave. How do you cook for yourself?"

"I eat at the diner almost every day. Half the time Angel doesn't charge me because I really don't eat that much. And you'd be surprised what you can make in the microwave." The look on her face pleaded with him.

"Please, Hart. Don't get all worked up. You're the only one who knows about this, and I'd like to keep it that way. It's too embarrassing."

Hart closed his eyes with shame, knowing she had been going through this all alone. He should have done something sooner—if he had known the truth. "Why didn't you tell me? Why have you been keeping this a secret from all your friends and me?"

Her eyes were downcast as if she struggled to find an answer. "I don't know. I guess I thought it would only be for a week or two. And then the weeks turned into months, and it just became my new normal. I'm used to being on my own, Hart. It's no big deal."

He reached toward her, pushing her dark hair behind her ear. The way she looked back at him made his heart leap in his chest. "Do you have any idea how dangerous this area is?" he asked quietly, cupping her cheek. "You've been coming here late after working all those damn entertainment jobs. What if some homeless guy from the park followed you or someone tried to carjack you in the parking lot? You know Atlanta is a huge hub for human trafficking. What if you were taken against your will by some predator? *It's not safe here,* Gia. You've got to know that. You've got to know the truth that your business has no future here either."

He struggled to get the words out, but she needed to know. Everyone he had talked to in the real estate market told him he was crazy to think he could get a buyer on board to revamp the area into something more desirable. The research was dismal. It was one of the highest crime-ridden areas in the state of Georgia. No one would come near this property with a ten-foot pole.

"I know." Her body language deflated. "I've just been putting off the inevitable. But don't forget, I grew up around here. People know me. They knew my Aunt Caroline. I like to think they've been looking out for me all these years."

"I'm sure your friends look out for you. I don't doubt that for a second. But you're a beautiful woman coming back here in the dead of night. It's not safe." He shook his head in disbelief. They really were from opposite sides of the tracks. He could never, ever relate to her situation, having grown up the way he did. But he was determined to help no matter how much she refused.

"I'm not leaving you here. I want you to move in with me, Gia."

She looked up at him, her mouth gaping. "*Live* with you? That's not even your home, Hart. It's your sister's condo. What would she have to say about that?"

He smiled, knowing his sister, Katie, would insist. "She won't take no for an answer." Pulling her chair toward him, he placed both of his hands on her thighs and squeezed. "I've been ready to start looking for my own place anyway. It's time." He tilted his head and gazed into her face. "Maybe we could look for a new place…together?"

***

Gia's neck muscles tightened and her heart pounded. She was overwhelmed but exhilarated by Hart's offer to move in with him. She told him she'd have to think about it but agreed to stay with him at his sister's condo—for the time being. It wasn't like her to give up control over a situation, but in this case, she consented. A large suitcase sat on the passenger side front seat along with several hanging clothes she had thrown on top. Following his car in the night, she was relieved that he knew her truth—relieved that she wouldn't have to spend another night alone.

By the time they unloaded her things, it was nearly two in the morning—the long, emotional day taking its toll. She looked forlornly at her meager belongings in the foyer and didn't have the energy to do anything more. Hart, on the other hand, seemed energized, bouncing around the condo with excitement, obviously happy she was there.

131

"Come here," he said with a broad smile on his face.

Shuffling her feet, she approached him. He laced his fingers through her hair and kissed her long and hard, a faint flicker of want spread through her body. Smoothing her bangs to the side, he gazed into her eyes. "Welcome to your new home."

Staring into his deep brown eyes, she couldn't help the relieved smile that blossomed across her face before laying her head sleepily on his chest. The feeling of peace that followed as his strong hands massaged the back of her neck and shoulders eased the tension in her body as her eyes fluttered closed in exhaustion.

"What time is your first class tomorrow?" he asked, hugging her tighter, his protective warmth penetrating her body as she snuggled against him.

"Three," she mumbled into his shirt.

"Good, you can sleep in. I'll be up early. I've got a meeting first thing, but I won't wake you. I want you to make yourself at home. Rearrange the closet and drawers and unpack your suitcase. If you have any boxes you want to start bringing over, we can store them in the walk-in closet. We'll figure it out."

"Mmhummm…" The steady rhythm of his heart beating was lulling her to sleep.

"Come on. Let's go to bed."

When Gia woke the next morning, Hart was already gone. She slowly sat up and stretched, feeling better than she had in months thanks to a good night's sleep in a real bed. She looked around the spotless room filled with morning light and sighed. Her life had taken a definite turn. Meeting Hartford Parker was probably the best thing that ever happened to her. The years of being alone and making tough decisions on her own had finally taken a toll—and she was tired. For him to take the reins and take her off the path of loneliness and isolation was a gift from the heavens. But his offer to move in together was huge. It was a life-changing decision that most couples made when they were in love.

Love.

Did she love him? Did he love her? They had never said those words out loud to each other. Never even close. But his actions were affectionate and sincere. He had once told her he adored her while they were making love, but nothing close to the L-word. She needed to sit him down and have a heart to Hart to discuss what their future entailed. Sifting through her suitcase, she grabbed some clothing and her toiletry bag before heading into the bathroom to get ready for the day.

An hour later, she was standing in the office of the pawn shop begging for more time.

"Please, I need another month to come up with the money. After I close the studio, I won't have to make any more lease payments, which will free up a lot of cash. Please."

The shop owner calmly shook his head as he eyed her. "We had an agreement Ms. Bates, and I've already extended it twice. I have a qualified buyer, and I'm ready to sell."

Gia's heart fell, and she closed her eyes.

"I'll tell you what. I'll give you until the end of business on Monday. That's the best I can do. Maybe you can find a friend or someone to loan you the money over the weekend."

She quickly looked up at the owner and grinned. "Thank you! Thank you so much!" Before he changed his mind, she was out the door with newfound determination. "I'll be back on Monday for sure," she yelled over her shoulder.

When she got to her car, her euphoria began to flail. How in the hell was she going to come up with two-thousand dollars by Monday? Donna was moving to Savannah over the weekend, and she owed her one last paycheck before she left. Ed Smith would be coming by any day as well because it was the first of the month and she owed him rent. Could she be bold enough to ask Hart for the money after everything he had already done for her? The very thought made her sick to her stomach. Old habits die hard and her independent attitude forged ahead, a tiny idea she had tucked away in her brain resurfacing.

"Franko Bartelli," she whispered. She knew what she had to do.

***

"The lease abstract is due next week before bids can go out to the contractors," Stephen Kaufman dictated across the large conference table. "Make sure the original lease is executed beforehand."

"Right." Hart scribbled notes on a large pad in front of him, thankful that his first big deal with the new firm was about to be signed. It hadn't taken him very long to negotiate a lucrative contract, a testament to his knowledge and abilities in the real estate business.

"So, any plans for the weekend?" When Hart looked up, Stephen was grinning from ear to ear as he leaned back in the leather chair. He knew that mischievous look by now.

"Uh, well. My girlfriend and I are probably gonna look at some property. We're moving in together."

"Good for you, lucky bastard!" Stephen congratulated him. He leaned forward with his hands clasped together. "While you and your girl are out and about real estate shopping, do you mind doing me a favor?"

Hart was afraid to ask. "What kind of favor?"

"I need you to cover for me in case Jessica calls looking for me, not that she will. I'd feel better leaving her with an emergency contact."

"Cover for what?"

Stephen looked at the closed door before continuing. "I'm taking Traci to my mountain house this weekend— you know, for a little fun." He winked wickedly and licked his lips, making Hart's skin crawl.

"I don't know…"

"Oh, come on! You get it, don't you? You, of all people." He swiveled in his chair and looked at him with narrowed eyes. "Traci is *hot*, and I need to get away for the weekend; away from the screaming children and my trashed house. The girls are driving me crazy at home. I can't think straight, and Jessica has unrealistic expectations when I'm around. I need this getaway, Hart."

"But isn't Jessica your *wife*, Mr. Kaufman?" Hart interrupted, calling his boss by his formal name.

Stephen shook his head. "I thought you were a team player Mr. Parker. Perhaps I was mistaken."

With a heavy sigh and hooded eyes, Hart felt his past guilt rear its ugly head and relented. "I am, Stephen. What exactly do you want me to do?"

GEORGIA ON MY MIND

CHAPTER EIGHTEEN

Steam rose from the pasta and sauce covering Hart's plate. Gia watched him shyly, as if anticipating his reaction to when he took his first bite. Twirling the fork around the noodles loaded with chicken and alfredo sauce, he opened his mouth wide and savored the dish. There was just the right amount of butter and cream, the rich parmesan cheese almost sweet on his tongue.

"Oh. My. God," he said with his mouth full.

"You like it?" She waited on pins and needles for his response.

He finished chewing and wiped his face with a linen napkin. "That's the best chicken alfredo I've ever had!" She blushed, biting her lower lip. "Seriously, where did you learn to make this?"

Forking a bite, Gia replied, "It's my Aunt Caroline's recipe. It was my favorite meal she made for me on special occasions."

He reached across the table and covered her hand with his. "What's the occasion tonight?"

She looked at him square in the face. "I'm happy."

Hart inhaled sharply. "Well, sweet thing, happy looks good on you."

The woman sitting across from him made him feel things he had never felt before. Knowing she was waiting for him back at the condo while stuck in atrocious Atlanta traffic made the commute almost bearable. He was happy too.

Gia had finished her classes by 5:30 p.m. and had texted him shortly after, telling him not to worry about dinner. She had even suggested he take his time getting home so she could serve him something special, as a thank you for taking her in. When he walked through the door, aromatic smells of garlic bread and pasta baking in the oven greeted him. A bottle of his favorite wine accompanied the special meal, which touched him deeply. As they conversed and ate at the romantic table filled with small candles, Hart couldn't help but feel a deep satisfaction when she was in his presence and knowing she was safe was very gratifying. He was excited about looking at property with her over the weekend. This was the start of a new life—for both of them.

"I talked with Ed Smith today. Told him this would be the last month for Dance Atlanta. He seemed to take it pretty well."

Hart set his fork to the side of his plate. "Are you okay? That's a big decision."

"It's the right decision. I've been putting it off for a long time. Your real estate information kind of sealed the deal. You were right. That whole area is gonna get worse before it gets any better. It's time to pull out."

He nodded in agreement. "You'll find your way. Have you thought about what you might want to do? Maybe teach at a bigger studio in the trendier areas? God, any studio would be thrilled to have a talented teacher like you, especially with your background and your time on *So You Think You Can Dance*. We could also look at securing another lease so you could move your entire business. It might be expensive, but if it's something you want to continue to do, I'm behind you 100 per cent. I'd be happy to be an investor."

She smiled warmly and took a sip of wine. "I think I need a break from being a business owner. I appreciate your offer, though. I called Ethan to give him a heads up, and he immediately told me about the upcoming show at the City Springs Theatre he needs some help with. Choreography, rehearsals… it could be something right up my alley while I think about what's next."

Hart beamed. "That's fantastic! What a great friend!"

Gia agreed. "He wants me to come by tomorrow night after my gig—introduce me to the dancers in the chorus at the tail end of rehearsal. I know you don't want me playing Marilyn anymore, but I need to honor the last few contracts I still have for gigs. It's only a couple more weekends. Are you okay with that?"

She was asking him if he was okay with it. Honestly, he wasn't. But he would handle a couple of more weekends if that's what she needed to do. He couldn't believe how quickly she had already started making plans. She was a go-getter. "You do whatever you think is right, sweetheart. I'm proud of you for coming up with a plan. And don't forget, I'll be right here waiting for you." She offered him a smile that made his manhood stir, her blue eyes breathtakingly beautiful in the candlelight.

"Did you get enough to eat?" she asked huskily.

"Mmm, yes. I'm stuffed."

"I hope you made room for dessert."

He watched as she slowly unbuttoned her shirt, a grin spreading across his face.

"What are you doing?" he asked, knowing exactly what she was up to.

"I'm getting ready."

"For dessert?"

"Yes."

She took the blouse off and stood, pulling down her pants. When she was in nothing but a lacy bra and panties, she walked around the table and stood in front of him with one hand on his shoulder. Her hips started to swing slowly back and forth, making Hart chuckle. "Are you dancing for me?"

"Mmmhumm," she smiled demurely, allowing the straps of her bra to fall to the side. "Can you unhook me please?" She turned around and sat on his lap, arching her back, making him gasp. He ran his fingertips lightly down her porcelain skin before unhooking the garment. She turned around, holding it against her chest while stifling a smile by biting her lower lip.

"God almighty, you're gorgeous." He drank in her playful image as she tossed the bra across the room, her breasts bouncing in front of his face. Pulling her forward, his mouth landed on her nipples and he began sucking and tugging them with his lips and tongue, making her moan. He kissed her neck up to her cheeks before his mouth consumed hers, their passion igniting a wildfire. She gyrated against him, and he used his free hand to slide down her belly to under the waistband of her panties, dipping his fingers into her hot seam. She pulled back and gripped his shoulders, locking eyes with him, the wetness between her legs suggesting he continue and bring her to a climax.

"Don't stop," she requested, her nostrils flaring with each puff of air she took in as she moved faster against his hand.

"I'll never stop," he promised, watching her come undone in his lap. He beheld her beauty at that moment and felt her tense for a quick second before shuddering in release.

***

That night was a turning point for Gia. She did everything in her power to show Hart how she honestly felt about him minus the vocalized words, "I love you." It was a test of sorts, to see if he might say it first. No one had ever said those words to her, not even her own selfish mother or her caring aunt. Sure, she felt loved by her Aunt

Caroline, but for some reason, her own family wasn't conditioned to say it. Love was a serious game changer for her, and she knew once she said those words out loud, there would be no turning back. Love was something she had coveted her entire life. Forget being raised by a stripper-drug-addict of a mother, or navigating financial ruin on her own. Being on the cusp of falling in love was the scariest thing she had ever been through.

After their little dessert session in the dining room, Hart took her to bed, and they made slow, sweet love for hours. The euphoria she felt through connecting with him on such an intimate level was overwhelming. There was a split second when she thought he was about to say those desirable words, causing her pulse to race faster than Ethan tap dancing at top speed. But he didn't say them. He told her he "loved making love to her." Not wanting to show her disappointment, she concentrated on the best lovemaking she had ever experienced, but it was very hard. For some reason, she was becoming desperate to hear him say it. She needed to know once and for all if Hartford Parker was in love with her. In her mind, if he said those words, she wouldn't go through with her weekend plan. She would trust him fully and finally divulge her secret about the ring asking *him* for the money. Asking him would finally relieve her of the armor she had built up around her heart.

Sitting in the dark family room and wrapped in a silk robe, she fingered a small glass of cognac while waffling over her decision. If Hart ever found out what she was about to do, he'd never forgive her, and she'd surely lose him forever. He had boldly told her he didn't want her working for the entertainment company anymore. And here she was contemplating working at Franko's strip club. The ghost of her mother was taunting her, and she was struggling. This was a two-show fix, not a career choice like it was for her mom. She was nothing like that woman—or was she? A handsome and successful guy like

Hart couldn't be linked to a stripper. He was from an upper-class family and was thriving in his lucrative career. What would his family and co-workers say if this ever got out? Would it be the old "like-mother-like daughter" mentality?

She had already fibbed by telling him she was helping out her friend Ethan with a show over the weekend. It wasn't a total lie because Ethan had suggested she think about reviving her dance career. If she could just get through the weekend and get her Aunt Caroline's ring back in her possession, she promised herself she'd never lie to him again and never, ever set foot in Franko's club. What he didn't know wouldn't hurt him, and she planned to keep it that way.

Franko Bartelli was chomping at the bit to get her on his stage. His offer still stood, and he promised to pay her up front before one inch of her body was exposed to the masses. She decided to play an iconic character on stage, much like her Marilyn and Madonna gigs. At least when she was acting, she could keep her emotions in check. The thought of being naked and on display in a room full of strangers made her nauseous, and she still wasn't sure how she was going to go through with it. The worst part was knowing she'd be following in her own mother's footsteps, succumbing to the sordid lifestyle for the quick money. For years, Ruby Bates danced in the dark confines of the popular clubs, abusing drugs and her body for financial gain. After Gia was born illegitimately, Ruby tried to quit the business and change her ways. But old habits die hard. Gia remembered strange men often coming to their home—her mother's "friends" as she called them. The loud music, laughter, and moaning behind the closed bedroom door became the soundtrack to her childhood.

"Two nights…" she whispered into the dark. Two nights, and this would be behind her and the memories of her late mother laid to rest. She was ready to move on with Hart and live happily ever after.

The liquor burned going down her throat as she blinked back tears. Shame covered her like a thick fog, making her head throb. She swore she would never be anything like her late mother. Here she was on the precipice of a new and exciting life with the man of her dreams, and she was about to play a game of Russian roulette. Her life had already changed dramatically in the past twenty-four hours. How much more could it change over the weekend if he found out? She'd be homeless for sure. A homeless, destitute *stripper*. She brought her hand up to her mouth to stifle a sob.

"Sweetie, what is it? What's going on?"

Hart was suddenly kneeling in front of her in bare feet, wearing nothing but his boxers. His hair was disheveled, and his hands were firmly gripping her thighs. She stiffened and quickly set the glass down on the side table, trying to regain her composure.

"I didn't mean to scare you. I woke up and reached for you. When you weren't there, I had to find you. Are you okay?"

Sniffling, she gripped his hand. "I'm...fine. I couldn't sleep. I...I didn't want to wake you."

His face appeared shadowed, the moon casting a blue light across his chiseled features. "Why can't you sleep? What's on your mind? At dinner, you said you were happy." He paused. "Why do I get the impression that something happened and now you're unhappy?" He hoisted himself up and sat beside her.

She sighed heavily. "I am happy, Hart. But to be perfectly honest with you, I guess I'm a little sad too. Not only am I closing the doors on Dance Atlanta, but I'm also closing the doors on a huge chapter of my life. I know I'm sentimental, but my emotional attachment to the place caught me off guard."

He seemed to relax and put his arm around her, holding her close. "I understand. That place has been a constant in your life since you were very young. Of course, you're sentimental."

She nodded in the dark.

"You need to have some sort of celebration before you close the doors. Maybe a 'going-away' party for your students? Something to commemorate the time you had there."

She nodded again. "That could be fun...or extremely depressing."

Hart chuckled in the darkness. "Concentrate on the great memories you have, not on what you've lost, sweet thing. If anything, you've gained something in this transition in your life."

"Really? What would that be?"

"Me."

A tingling sensation filled her body.

"I hope you know how much I care for you, Gia. You've changed my life," he said softly.

Her heart started to race. Could this be the moment she had been waiting for? "I care about you too, Hart. I don't know what I would do without you."

They clung to each other in silence, the anticipation of hearing those words she desperately needed to hear fading into the night. The stillness was a sign to her. A sign she was to move ahead and do the unthinkable to save the only heirloom left from her family. She had lost so much in her life. She wasn't about to let her aunt's ring slip through her fingers if there was something she could do about it. Unfortunately, it was something so awful and demeaning, she couldn't dwell, or she'd be a blubbering idiot for sure.

"I'm tired now," she muttered.

"Let's get you back to bed." They stood, and the two of them walked to the bedroom, holding hands.

CHAPTER NINETEEN

The entire day was a blur. Gia finished her classes, going through the motions as if she were a robot on autopilot. Knowing Hart had already made plans that night made things a little more comfortable. At least he'd be out-of-pocket and preoccupied with his friends while she'd be doing the unthinkable.

"What'll ya have tonight? Egg salad? We've got a baked chicken special going on too if you need some protein." Her gal-pal, Angel, stood on the other side of the counter with her hand on her hip. The diner was bustling with Friday night regulars as the time approached the dinner hour.

"No, Angel. I'm not hungry. Some black coffee, please."

Angel scowled. "Black coffee? For dinner? I won't be havin' any of that. Let me fix you up with our special."

Gia shook her head and smiled. "No thanks. I've got to head out soon. Big show tonight."

"Uh-huh…" Angel put her hand on her hip. "You're a little off. What's going on?"

Leave it to one of her best friends to read her like a book. Gia was a nervous wreck trying to gather the courage to head over to Franko Bartelli's club and get ready for the evening ahead. Was it that obvious she was out of sorts?

"I'm fine, Angel. Really."

"Did you and Mr. Wonderful have a fight?"

She chuckled. "No. Me and Mr. Wonderful are doing just fine. He's out tonight with some friends celebrating his buddy's bachelor party."

Angel rolled her eyes. "Oh, Lord! What is it with guys and their bachelor parties? I'm sure your lover-boy is gonna come home reeking of whiskey and cigars with some poor strippers g-string stuffed in his pocket." She let out a wallop of laughter as Gia shifted uncomfortably in her chair.

"No. It's not like that. Hart's friends rented some lanes at the local bowling alley. It's quite tame." She watched as Angel poured her a mug of steaming coffee.

"If you say so. You're not performing your Marilyn for any bachelor parties tonight, are you?" Her eyes showed humor in her expression.

Gia stirred some sugar into her drink. "Ha! Wouldn't that be hysterical?" Angel snorted as she walked away to pick up a food order, leaving Gia to ponder the night ahead. Her costume and makeup bag were already in the car; the music for her routine loaded on a flash drive tucked into her purse.

When Angel came back, she pursed her lips. "I know you're up to something. Spill it." She crossed her arms over her ample bosom.

Gia sighed, shifting her thoughts. "I'm closing Dance Atlanta…"

"What? Oh, girl. I'm so sorry." The look she gave was full of empathy.

"It's time. Donna just moved away, and I'm losing students left and right. It's okay." She sipped the hot coffee nervously, hoping this news would appease her friend and get her to stop asking questions.

"Well, you've done the best you could in the circumstances; you've had a great run." Angel paused. "Were you ever able to get your aunt's ring back?"

The coffee suddenly felt like paste sliding down her throat, and she coughed. "I'm getting it back on Monday. I'll have all the money by the end of the weekend."

"Well, there's some good news!" Angel's face lit up, her broad smile exposing the gap between her front teeth. "I'm so glad. I know how much that ring means to you."

Gia nodded quickly and started to stand. If she didn't get out of there, she knew she'd cave and tell Angel what she was about to do. "I gotta run. Big night ahead. Wish me luck."

"Girl. You don't need no luck!"

***

The mechanical pinsetter lifted, revealing the perfectly aligned white pins standing erect like little wooden men in a formation. Hart grinned, knowing he was about to win this round. He brought the bright, red bowling ball up to his chin before moving forward with purpose, throwing the circular twelve-pound weight underhand. It glided effortlessly across the long narrow lane hitting the center pin with a loud thwack knocking every single one of them over with a crash.

"*Strike!*" he yelled enthusiastically, thrusting his arms up into the air in a victory pose. His buddy, Mitch Montgomery, shoved a drink in his hand while patting him aggressively on the back.

"Dude! That's the game!"

The group of friends talked loudly among the music and the crashing of pins in neighboring lanes of the recently renovated bowling alley. The smell of fresh popcorn wafted through the air as the overhead monitor displayed a brightly colored graphic of a dynamite explosion with the bold letters, STRIKE. The entire group had kept in touch since high school, several of them ending up at the same college. It was a brotherhood of sorts, each guy holding a special place in one another's lives. Mitch was having a destination wedding in less than a week—only close family invited. He planned a guy's night so they could celebrate and appease his group of disappointed friends who wouldn't be a part of his nuptials.

Taking a break from bowling, they sat in a circle on hard plastic chairs, gulping pitchers of cheap draft beer and recounting stories of their youth. Their conversations were loud and raucous, and the bartender brought out several rounds of shots, tiny glasses raised in unison among friends.

"Cheers to Mitchy, our pal forever."

"Cheers!" they said in unison.

The bowling resumed, and Mitch leaned over, speaking very closely to Hart. "When are you gonna let everyone know about your new girl? What was her name again?"

Hart finished tying the multi-colored bowling shoe that had come loose and sat up. "Gia. I will. Not tonight, though. Tonight is all about you, brother."

Mitch grinned and licked his lips. "I still can't believe Gia was Marilyn at my birthday party."

"Yeah. Well, she's super-talented and helping choreograph a show at the City Springs Theatre now. I think her Marilyn days are finally gonna be behind her."

"I'm sure you're happy about that. I'd die if Sophie did a strip-tease for some strange guy at a party. Not that what Gia did was in bad taste or anything. I get it. She's a performer. She did a great job."

"Thanks." Hart had told Mitch in confidence that he was seriously dating Gia. He had yet to introduce his new girlfriend to his close circle of friends, knowing that some of them would question his choice because of her dancing gigs. Mitch was different. He was loyal and never judged, standing by him during the whole firing debacle in DC and Hart was grateful.

"Is it serious? You seem happier these days, dude."

Hart smirked before nodding. "Yeah, man. I think it is serious."

"That's awesome. You deserve the kind of happiness that me and Sophie share."

Hart leaned in. "How did you know, Mitch? How did you know Sophie was 'the one'?"

Mitch smiled. "I don't know. It's weird, but… you just know. You want to… take care of them. Spoil them." He paused in thought. "Your heart races when you know you're gonna see her, and you're sad when you have to leave her. Does that make any sense?"

Hart knew precisely what he meant. "Yeah. Total sense."

"Looks like my buddy, Hartford Parker, is finally in love." Mitch slapped Hart on the back. "Let's finish up here and grab a drink someplace else. Whadyasay?"

Hart grinned, knowing his friend had hit the nail on the head. "Whatever you want. It's your night!"

***

Gia concentrated on lining the bottom rim of her eyes in a smoky shade. Her hands shook so badly, she had to stop several times before she gave up and threw the pencil at her reflection in the mirror.

"What's wrong darlin'? Nerves gettin' to ya?" A very tall and voluptuous woman wearing a terrycloth robe and sky-high pumps leaned against the long edge of the makeup mirrors. Her crimson nails tipped with tiny white crystals twinkled in the bright vanity mirror lights, and her dramatic eyelashes hooded her dark eyes. She had introduced herself earlier as Charity. Apparently, she was a regular at the club and a mentor to the new girls on the floor. "I've got something to take the edge off if you want it—"

"No, thanks," Gia interrupted. She knew most of these girls probably did drugs. How could they not? The thumping music inside the club reverberated in the dressing room, syncing with her own thumping heart.

"Well, I'll just leave it right here in case you change your mind." She placed a tiny white pill on the back edge. "Franko says you're the real deal—a genuine trained dancer. He says you'll put us all to shame." Her smile was snide.

Gia felt heat rush to her cheeks and shook her head quickly. "I don't know about that."

"Well, I'm looking forward to your act. Franko says it's very theatrical—an homage to Prince. I just love Prince."

Gia couldn't help but stare at Charity's over-glossed lips that were the shade of bright pink bubblegum. She seemed kind enough, but Gia knew better. Growing up with a mother who did this for a living gave her an advantage, keeping her on her toes. Most of these girls were either down on their luck like her or addicted to drugs and the easy money. Thank God, after two shows, it would all be behind her, and she would never have to go through something like this again. The thought of being naked in front of a live audience in less than two hours was causing her to come unhinged, and she still wasn't sure if she could go through with it. She was standing on a ledge looking down at the unknown, about ready to jump.

"I guess you'll have to wait and see." She eyed the pill. "What is that anyway?"

Charity smiled, causing one thin eyebrow to arch playfully. "Valium. It'll calm you right down."

Gia's eyebrow raised in response as her phone started to buzz. "Excuse me, Charity."

"No problem."

Lifting the phone, she could see it was Hart trying to call. Panicking, she held her breath and wondered for a split-second if he knew exactly where she was. She didn't dare answer and quickly shoved the phone into her bag. The last thing she needed was to break down and spill her guts before show time. "What he doesn't know won't hurt him," she whispered, trying to convince herself as she looked straight at her reflection. Taking a quick look around, her eyes fell on the pill Charity had left behind. One Valium wouldn't hurt her. She remembered her friend Angel being prescribed some after her car accident. It seemed to keep her relaxed and calm during her recovery. Perhaps it could do the same for her tonight. Without thinking it through further, she grabbed the pill and shoved it into her mouth, chasing it with a weak gin and tonic.

"Fuck," she said as she dropped her head into her open hands. This was exactly like mother-like-daughter. This was rock bottom.

GEORGIA ON MY MIND

CHAPTER TWENTY

The guys loaded into two Suburban's and left the bowling alley, pulling into the dismal Atlanta Friday night traffic. Disappointed, Hart clicked off his phone and held it on his lap. His friend Mitch was right. He was in love with Gia. When the realization hit him over the head like a baseball bat, all he wanted to do was tell her. He wanted to say the words, "I love you" to Gia Bates. When she didn't answer her phone, he assumed she was probably in the middle of her Marilyn act. He smiled, thinking back to that first night when she came waltzing into the country club dining room in her Monroe get-up. Little did he know she was the one who would steal his heart. On a whim, he decided to text those three little words to her. Maybe when she was finished performing, his words might cheer her up after all she had been going through and finally help her to decide if she wanted to move in with him once and for all. He couldn't blame her for being cautious; after all, she had been on her own for most of her life. Perhaps his text would set things straight in her mind, and she'd say, "yes" to being with him on a permanent basis.

"What are you doing, man?" Mitch eyed Hart's phone.

"Sending Gia a message. Something I should have told

her last night." He hit the send button and leaned back contentedly, ready to celebrate. "Where are we going anyway?"

Mitch grinned while another friend chimed in, "*White Satin*. It wouldn't be a real bachelor party without going to a strip club!"

"Sophie's not going to be happy about this!" Mitch bemoaned loudly. "But I guess I don't have a choice, do I?" All the guys in the car whooped and hollered, the alcohol they had consumed earlier giving everyone a healthy buzz.

Hart looked out the window as the car service pulled into the VIP drop-off of the club, illuminated with dramatic up-lighting. Over the years, he had been to countless strip clubs, never giving it a second thought. Tonight, however, was different. Knowing Gia's story about her mother and her upbringing hit too close to home. He wasn't sure if going in would be appropriate, especially after telling Gia he loved her. This certainly wasn't showing any love for her.

"Come on. You got my back; I got yours. Just a couple of drinks and we'll call it a night." Mitch grabbed him by the forearm as if sensing his hesitation and hoisted him out of the car.

The music was thumping, and the place was packed. A cloud of smoke hung in the air in the dark confines of the building. Scantily dressed cocktail waitresses arrived at their VIP table in an instant, flirting and batting their eyes at the crew of well-dressed, upper-class Atlanta men who had just arrived. Whiskey shots and cigars were ordered and delivered in record time, the alcohol traveling down Hart's throat soothing his nerves. A trio of topless ladies danced and swung on silver poles on the stage while the first few rows of rowdy men waved money in the air, urging them to take it all off. If Gia knew he was here, she'd never forgive him. This foul place had been a sad reality in her young life, stealing her mother away and into the arms of sex, drugs, and greed. He felt nauseous and wanted to leave.

"Wait! Where are you going?" Mitch stood, blocking his escape.

"I gotta piss, man. I'll be right back."

Mitch tilted his head and narrowed his eyes. Hart nodded and smiled. "I'll be right back," he said reassuringly. As he slowly made his way to the front of the house, the music stopped, and the lights dimmed. A low rumbly voice came over the speakers.

"Ladies and gentlemen, *The White Satin* is pleased to introduce a new Satin Doll in our lineup this evening. Please welcome... Miss Georgia B."

The little hairs on the back of Hart's neck stood straight up. Slowly, he turned around with wide eyes and watched as a woman came out to the center of the stage. She posed under a single spotlight, one long leg pointed out from her side, one hand on her hip and the other hand splayed behind an embellished purple fedora hat with black lace trim hiding her face. She was wearing purple stilettos and a dramatic purple waistcoat adorned with crystals that shimmered in the hot light. A white, high-collar satin shirt layered with chiffon ruffles peeked from behind the theatrical coat covering her entire upper body. The only exposed skin was on her long, sky-high dancer's legs. He could recognize those legs anywhere.

The thumping bass and keyboard of the familiar Prince tune, *The Beautiful Ones* started, and she began to move effortlessly on stage to whoops and hollers from the crowd. A smoke machine had been turned on, and billows of soft plumes poured out from behind purple LED lighting upstage. Hart held his breath, his hands fisting at his sides, not sure how to react. She was mesmerizing to watch, hypnotizing him, making him freeze in place. Several patrons bumped into him as he stood motionless in the aisle, unable to take his eyes off her.

She peeled the jacket off, revealing her bare arms in the

sleeveless, high-collar shirt. When she suddenly grabbed at the ruffles and jerked them to the side, he was jolted wide awake staring at her crystal-encrusted bra underneath. Kicking and moving her hips seductively, she had the entire audience in a trance. When she finally flung the fedora off, revealing her dark, bobbed hair and dramatic blue eyes, Hart couldn't take it anymore. He bolted toward the stage only to be met by a very large, ebony-skinned man who stopped him in his tracks.

"No, sir. No touching the Satin Dolls." The big house-of-a-man grabbed him gruffly by the arm and started to escort him to a side door. His buddy Mitch was by his side in an instant.

"Dude! What's going on?" he yelled over the loud music.

Hart panicked, looking over his shoulder at the stage. Gia was in nothing but her bra and g-string at this point, Prince screaming the lyrics of the iconic song in painful angst as the crowd hollered with pleasure. Without a second thought, Hart started yelling and punching at the man who held him, trying to get away. Several blows hit the guy in the face.

"Gia! Gia! Stop—don't do this!"

Startled by his familiar voice, she squinted in the bright light and looked around, shading her eyes with her hand, stopping the performance. The crowd started to boo.

"Gia! Over here! Stop!" he suddenly broke free and was almost to the stage when out of the blue, a massive fist met his face with a *bam*, sending a shock of instant pain to his cheek. He stumbled before his eyes rolled back into his head and he saw stars.

*

Gia knew it was Hart's voice she had heard. She could barely make out the commotion near the front of the stage, the Prince song continuing to blast in her ears among the hazy fog in the building. Her chest was heaving with adrenaline as she tried to figure out what was happening, the crowd of patrons egging her on to continue. With shaking hands, she bent down and picked up the costume pieces she had thrown off and gathered them in her arms. Her once active muscles felt like pudding, the Valium she had taken earlier not helping at the moment. Quickly, she darted stage right, straight into the arms of Franko Bartelli. He was not happy.

"You're not finished, doll. The song's not over." He eyed her menacingly up and down, his fingertips digging into the white flesh of her arm. Grabbing the stuff out of her arms, he pushed her back onto the stage. She stumbled before regaining her balance and stood in the brightness of the spotlight, feeling as if she were already naked and exposed. Glancing back at Franko, he gave her a reassuring nod. Trembling, she bent over and very slowly, took off her shoes as if it were a part of her act. Looking at Franko one last time, she cursed under her breath before she ran to the other side of the stage and made a beeline for the dressing room, locking the door behind her. Very quickly, she shoved her clothes into a bag and grabbed her purse. Franko was cursing and pounding on the door.

"Georgia! Get the fuck out here right now! *Georgia*!"

There was no escaping. The only way out was through the door she had come in. Backing up to the farthest corner, she gripped her possessions at her chest and slid down the wall to the floor in defeat. She had ruined everything good in her life. It was over.

Music continued to thump from the stage and she wondered who had stepped in to save the day. Was it sweet Charity? Maybe one of the other tattooed girls? The minutes ticked agonizingly by before a jangling of keys could be heard, and the door opened wide. She looked up and her eyes locked in on Hart. Drops of blood stained his white shirt, and a menacing bruise was noticeable across his face. His hair was disheveled and his expression morose. He slowly closed the door behind him.

Gia couldn't move and clutched her belongings to her

chest, shaking uncontrollably. She tensed as Hart approached and kneeled in front of her. His brow furrowed as he cupped her cheek and looked into her eyes with intensity.

"Just breathe," he said gently. "I know you're on something. I can see it in your eyes."

She closed her eyes tightly, wishing him away with all her might, hoping this was all a nightmare, and she was going to wake up soon. Keeping her eyes shut as if her life depended on it, she felt her belongings pulled from her grasp and could hear muffled voices in the room before strong hands pulled her up and carried her out. The thumping of the club dissipated, and she felt a soft blanket cover her in the backseat of a vehicle. When the car door slammed shut, she slumped in the seat and finally took in a breath, peeking through slit eyes out the window. *The White Satin* was getting smaller and smaller as the vehicle drove away. She continued to shudder uncontrollably, not sure if it was the temperature making her cold or if the pill she had taken was having an adverse effect on her system. Maybe it was the fact that she had been caught in yet another lie that she couldn't explain her way out of or maybe because she had been saved, yet again by Hartford Parker. Whatever it was, fear, relief, drugs, or temperature, she felt like she was on the verge of a meltdown.

Strong arms wrapped around her, making her gasp. She turned in alarm toward Hart's familiar handsome face.

"Shh, Gia. I'm here. You're okay."

Burying her head into his shoulder, she swallowed hard. "I think I'm gonna be sick…" Her voice was barely audible in her reply.

"Hey man! Pull over, so she doesn't throw up all over the back seat!" he yelled at the driver.

The SUV immediately came to a screeching halt. Hart threw open the door and quickly dragged her body over his lap so she could vomit on the street below. His warm hands were in her hair holding the edges back from her mouth as she gasped and retched. Gia started to sob, gripping his thigh, holding on for dear life. When she finally finished and could catch a breath, her head began to spin before everything went black.

GEORGIA ON MY MIND

CHAPTER TWENTY-ONE

The bed was soft and the faint sound of birds happily chirping could be heard coming from an open window. Gia swallowed before opening her eyes to the familiar bedroom. Quickly, she looked to the side, but Hart wasn't there. She sighed, her heart heavy with snapshots coming to mind from the previous night. How could she ever talk her way out of this? She had made a terrible, terrible mistake—one that her relationship with Hart would probably not survive.

Looking down at herself, she noticed she was wearing a sleeping shirt and underwear. Gone was the ruffled shirt and G-string from the night before. Someone must have dressed her. That someone must have been Hart. Her memory of the evening was fuzzy as she tried to recollect all that had happened, and she internally chastised herself for taking the Valium Charity had offered. It totally knocked her out. She should have known better. Staring out the window at the beautiful spring morning, a wave of regret came over her as she remembered Hart being in the audience and yelling for her to stop. Earlier, he had told her he was going to be with some guys celebrating their buddy Mitch's upcoming wedding. What were the chances they'd end up at the one strip club where she was performing? The odds were crazy, making her shake her head. If he was there, that meant his friends were there too and saw the whole thing unfold. Hanging her head in shame, she felt the weight of the world on her shoulders, knowing she had made a complete fool of herself; knowing she would be judged forever more because of one dreadful decision. There was no way someone like Hartford Parker would continue to date someone like her.

Her entire body felt like she had the flu as she got out of the bed and went into the bathroom. Staring at her reflection in the mirror, looking at her teased hair and the heavy show makeup remaining from the night before disgusted her. Her lipstick smudged across her cheek, and the eyeliner had muddled under her blue eyes, making her look very Goth. After scrubbing her face clean and brushing her hair, she packed up her toiletries and pulled her clothes out of the drawers, stuffing them into her suitcases she had stored in the walk-in closet. She knew she couldn't stay there any longer and wondered if she would even be able to teach her Saturday afternoon dance classes with the way she was feeling. Eyeing her purse on a chair, she rummaged through it to find her phone, intent on calling Ethan to see if he could help her out. She hit the home button on her cell phone and gasped.

I love you Gia. I just wanted you to know that. I can't wait to see you tonight so I can tell you in person.

Her eyes welled with tears, and she swiped at them so she could read the text message over and over again.

Hart loved her.

Pursing her lips, she sat on the bed sniffling, the timing of his text taking her aback. It had come through an hour before her performance last night. If she had just kept her phone out in the dressing room and looked at his message, everything would not have gone so terribly wrong. If she had just looked at her fucking phone, she would have seen his text and wouldn't have gone through with her performance. He loved her. It was exactly what she had wanted to hear.

She looked out the window again, trying to decide what to do next. The thought of seeing Hart made her uneasy. What would she say? What would he say? Surely, he had changed his mind about loving someone like her after last night, especially after embarrassing him in front of his closest friends. She tugged on some yoga pants and dared to open the door.

"Hart?" Her voice croaked when she spoke. There was no answer.

She padded down the stairs carefully and poked her head around the corner. There was no sign of him in the kitchen area. Looking further down the hallway, she could see him talking on his phone on the back porch. One hand was on his hip and he was pacing. Boldly, she opened the screen door and stepped out, his eyes widening at the sight of her.

"Yes, text me your address, and I'll be right over, okay?" He paused, looking her up and down, his expression deadpan. "No, Jessica. I don't mind. And please, don't call 9-1-1. I'm on my way." He rolled his eyes and started nodding. "Okay, okay. See you in a few. Bye."

Clicking off his phone, he put both hands on his hips and let out a huff of air. "We gotta go." He grabbed her hand, pulling her into the living room.

"Wha… what do you mean? Where? What's going on?"

"I'll tell you in the car. Get some shoes on. We gotta move fast!"

Gia sprinted up the stairs and grabbed her flip-flops and purse, being sure to lock the front door on her way out. Hart was already in his Mercedes, revving the engine as she got in.

"Buckle up," he requested, quickly pulling out of the condo complex. Gia did as she was told, realizing she was still wearing her sleeping shirt with no bra on. Wherever it was they were going, she prayed it was casual.

"So, I told you my boss is away this weekend with his mistress and gave his wife my number in case of an emergency."

"Yeah? What's going on?"

Hart clutched the steering wheel of the car speeding down the four-lane highway. She noticed his right cheek was stained with a sinister purple bruise and immediately felt remorse. "One of her daughters got her head caught in their staircase railing. She's stuck."

Gia couldn't help but let out a chuckle. "What?"

Hart glanced at her and grinned. "Yeah. Her head is stuck. Jessica called me in a panic asking if she should call 9-1-1."

"Oh, my god."

"I know, right? I told her to hold tight. She doesn't live that far, only a few miles up Highway 141 in the St. Ives subdivision. Pretty nice area. I'm sure the Kaufman's have a great big house." He turned and looked at her again. "I'm sorry this was so abrupt. How are you feeling?"

Gia flushed as heat rose on her neck. She looked down at her hands she was absentmindedly wringing in her lap. "I'm okay," she managed to say. "I'm sorry about last night. I can explain—"

"I don't want to talk about that now," he interrupted sternly. "There'll be plenty of time to talk about it later, Gia." She nodded forlornly and looked out the window as the weight of the world once again settled on her.

It only took ten minutes before they arrived at the secured subdivision. Hart punched in a code that opened the ornate gate and sped through the winding roads toward the Kaufman residence. As they pulled up a curved driveway that cut through the manicured lawn, Gia gasped at the sight of the palatial home. The stucco house was huge, the Kaufman's wealth obvious.

"Come on," Hart urged. They trotted to the front door, and he rang the bell. The sound of a child wailing echoed in the background.

Stephen Kaufman's wife Jessica answered the door, carrying a baby on her hip as two more little blonde heads peeked from around her tanned legs. "Thank God, you're here!" she sputtered, her Southern accent pronounced. "Jilly's on the back stairs in the kitchen. Come on!" She grabbed Hart's hand, pulling him through the foyer.

Gia followed and noticed right away that the home was in total disarray. Toys lay scattered in every room and dishes stacked up in the sink or on counters in the open kitchen. It was a little overwhelming.

"Here she is. My poor baby, Jilly," Jessica mimicked a baby voice, speaking directly to her young daughter as she bounced the other baby on her hip. Jilly's face was red as a beet as she kept trying to pull her head out of the wooden spokes of the railing, her nose snotty and her cheeks wet with tears. Blonde ringlets bounced each time she pulled back, trying to get unstuck and each time she couldn't, she let out a screeching wail.

"I don't know what happened. One minute, Jilly was playing happily with her little ponies and the next, her head was stuck smack in the center of these rails."

Gia got a good look at Jessica Kaufman. Her blonde hair piled on top of her head in a messy bun, and she wore black running shorts paired with a hot pink camisole on her thin frame. The young, blue-eyed mother didn't have a stitch of makeup on, her tanned face smattered with faint freckles across her nose. Even in her state of duress, she was drop-dead gorgeous.

Gia leaned down to be eye-level with the other two little girls standing by their mother. "Hi. My name's Gia. Why don't we go and play in the family room while Mr. Parker and your mommy take care of your sister, okay?" She turned to Jessica and held her hands out to take the baby. "Hey, Jessica. I'm so sorry we have to meet under these circumstances. Let me help you out and take the girls into the other room, so they're out of the way."

"Where are my manners? Yes, it's nice to meet you Gia. Stephen mentioned Hart was looking at property this weekend with his girlfriend." Her smile was authentic. If she only knew what had transpired the night before. "Here you go." She passed off her youngest daughter.

"Come on little one. What's your name?" Gia asked, wrapping her arms around the small tyke. She was heavier than Gia anticipated.

The oldest of the girls spoke up first. "That's JoAnne, but we call her Jo-Jo. She's almost one."

"I love that name! Hey, little Jo-Jo!" The baby offered a big grin, exposing two little teeth. "And what's your name?" she asked, turning to the oldest sibling.

"I'm Jennifer. I'm six, and this is Julia." She pointed to the wide-eyed little girl who was sucking her thumb. "She's four, but she doesn't talk much."

"Well, it's very nice to meet you Jennifer, Julia, and Jo-Jo."

The stuck little girl started to wail again as Hart was intently surveying the rails. "And let's not forget Jilly!" Gia shouted so she could hear. Her comment seemed to appease the child for a moment.

"Sweet little Jill is two years old," Jessica said, stroking her fair hair. "Four little babies six and under. What was I thinking?" She nervously laughed before changing the subject. "I just can't thank y'all enough for being here. I'm so, so sorry for takin' up your Saturday morning."

"No problem, Jessica. I'm glad we could help. I'll have your daughter out in no time."

Gia ushered the little girls into the family room and sat on the floor. The baby was content to stay in her lap and stared up at her with big blue eyes. Gia couldn't help but run her fingers through her baby-fine, silky hair. "Why don't you show me your favorite toys?"

*

Hart rummaged in the garage area Jessica had described and found what he was looking for. Taking the small saw

166

and hammer back inside, he couldn't help but overhear Gia chatting away with the little girls, causing him to stop for a moment and smile. She was good with children. It was evident the first time he saw her teaching a ballet class. She was in her element when she was around kids—not so much when she was around a bunch of drunk idiots shouting at her to take off all her clothes. His smile changed to a frown in an instant. They needed to talk about what had happened, but there had been no time. At least she was feeling better and was away from that hell-hole, the agony of watching her on stage something he never wanted to witness again. For her to come with him on this unexpected outing spoke volumes. She was willing—and she was with him.

Jessica was kneeling beneath her daughter, holding a straw to her tiny mouth that dipped into a cup of water. "Jilly was thirsty," she explained.

"I'd be thirsty too if my head were stuck," he teased. The little girl spotted the saw in his hands and started to flail, jerking her small head back and forth in fear.

"No! Baby, stop! He's not going to hurt you!" Jessica reassured the little girl.

Loud, high-pitched crying ensued, making Hart want to cover his ears. "Sweetheart, I'm gonna cut through this rail at the bottom here, see? It's not gonna touch you."

Jill looked down at the saw while holding onto two rails in a death grip with her small hands. Hart noticed her tiny fingernails were painted pink.

"There we go, nice and slow. Let's get you out of jail!"

The three of them watched the saw move carefully back and forth, the teeth of the blade causing bits of sawdust to float to the floor. When Hart was about halfway through, he pushed on the wooden spoke, and it cracked loose. Jill immediately freed herself and trotted down the stairs into her mother's arms.

"There, there my sweet silly Jilly. You're all right." She hoisted the little girl up onto her hip where she buried her nose in her neck. Stroking the back of her blonde curls, Jessica looked right at Hart. "I don't know what I would've done without you. You saved the day."

"I was glad to help." Peering behind Jessica's shoulder, he made eye contact with the little girl. "You okay?" She nodded, shyly clinging to her mother. "Good." He patted her head before collecting the tools he had used to free her. "Sorry about the railing. It's gonna need replacing."

"Oh, don't worry about that. I can call a handyman, or maybe Stephen can fix it if he's ever home."

Hart felt a pang of guilt, knowing exactly where Jessica's husband was. The bastard had left his poor wife alone with his four daughters when they should have been together as a family enjoying a lovely spring Saturday morning.

As they walked back toward the family room, Jessica paused. "I'm sure Stephen told you this, but I knew your sister Katie Parker at Lakeside High School very well. She was always the sweetest girl."

"Thanks. Katie is pretty special."

"I was on the cheerleading squad, and I remember you were quite the football player." She sighed. "Those were the days, weren't they?"

Hart nodded in agreement. "Glory days. Some of the best."

Jill wiggled out of her arms and ran into the family room with lightning speed, making the two adults laugh. "See? She's already over her little ordeal. Little girls can be very dramatic."

"Kids bounce right back, don't they?" He started to walk away but stopped when she touched his arm, looking at him poignantly.

"I know you work closely with my husband Stephen," she whispered.

Hart's eyes grew wide. "Yes. We work together."

Her cheeks blushed, and she nervously smiled. "Do you know where he is this weekend? He's not answering his phone or replying to my text messages. He told me before he left that he was going somewhere remote that didn't have good cell towers. That's why he gave me your number. But I can't help but wonder, wouldn't there be a landline?" The look of concern on her face made Hart avert his eyes with shame. "I mean, what if somethin' awful had happened to Jilly and I couldn't reach him. Can you reach him?"

He wasn't about to tell her Stephen was at their family mountain home in North Georgia probably fucking his mistress at that very moment. He knew the place had a landline because Stephen had given him the number, just in case.

"I'm sure he'll call and check in. You know how he is. A workaholic if you ask me." He chuckled unconvincingly.

Jessica tightened her lips and sighed. "Yeah. A workaholic."

GEORGIA ON MY MIND

CHAPTER TWENTY-TWO

After a quick round of donut holes and milk to celebrate Jilly's freedom, Gia and Hart started to leave. JoJo held her baby hands up, indicating to Gia she wanted to be held while Jennifer and Jill grabbed her legs, begging her not to go. Little Julia remained silent with her thumb stuck in her mouth and innocently grabbed Hart's hand. It was precious.

"Girls, let's not cause a scene. It's time for our guests to leave." Jessica sounded like a sweet school teacher trying to calm down her rowdy class. "Thanks again. For everything. And don't forget to put some aloe vera on that bruised cheek of yours. It'll clear it right up."

"Thanks for the tip." When Jessica had asked about his face, he fibbed, telling her he had bumped into a doorframe during the night. "If anything else comes up, give me a call. We'll be around all weekend," Hart replied. Jessica nodded, as if relieved she would have contact with at least some adults over the next couple of days.

Gia handed the baby back to Jessica. "Your daughters are so sweet. They're lucky to have you." Jo-Jo started to cry, reaching for Gia again.

"Ha! If you say so. Again, it was so nice to meet you.

Thank you for making such a great impression on my girls."

When they got in the car, Gia looked out the window one last time to see Jessica standing on the front stoop of the magnificent home surrounded by her beautiful daughters. The snapshot of the little family waving goodbye made her feel melancholy, knowing what her husband, Stephen was up to.

"He's such a dick!" she bemoaned.

"Yeah, I know."

They drove in silence as Hart navigated through the bustling traffic. Gia noticed his cheek was turning darker. "Is your face okay? Does it hurt?" she asked tentatively, wanting desperately to reach up and touch him.

He glanced at her and smirked. "I'm fine. One of the hazards of trying to beat off a guy who weighed twice as much as me, I suppose."

"Oh, Hart. I'm so sorry…"

He shook his head. "I don't even know how to begin this conversation."

"I know," she squeaked, feeling small and vulnerable.

"I mean, you lied to me. Again. Why would you do that?"

Gia licked her lips and tried to explain. "You have to know it was my very first time at the club. I was trying to make some quick money—"

"*I know!*" he interrupted loudly.

"What? How?" She watched him sigh deeply, his knuckles turning white as he forcefully gripped the steering wheel.

Gritting his teeth, he described what had transpired. "A huge fight broke out when I rushed the stage, but it didn't last long. When things calmed down, that damn owner, Bartelli refused to let me go backstage to get you. All he was interested in was getting some other poor girl out there performing for the crowd. Oh, and getting his check back from you. Two thousand dollars. I agreed to help him find it in your stuff, but first, he had to track down his night manager who had the keys to the dressing room you locked yourself in. I was out of my fucking mind worried about you. He told me everything—that you needed quick cash and had agreed to two shows at the club." He turned and looked straight at her. "What in the *hell* were you thinking? And what did you need that amount of money for?"

Gia crouched silently in the seat, humiliation filling her entire being.

"You choose to keep putting yourself in these dangerous situations, Gia. And the drugs? Why? Your own mother *died* from a drug overdose! Why would you do that? Is this another habit you've been keeping from me these past few months? Are you trying to follow in your mother's footsteps?"

"*No!*" she cried out.

The heated exchange was escalating, and Hart suddenly pulled his car into a grocery store parking lot, putting it in park and abruptly facing her. "Then why? Were you forced to take them?" His expression pleaded with her to tell the truth.

"No… No one forced me to do anything. I… I don't know why I took the Valium. I was stressed and upset… Charity told me it would calm me down. I just wanted to get through the night without falling apart." She watched Hart run both hands through his hair before laying his head back on the seat in exasperation. "The money was to get my Aunt Caroline's ring back from a pawn shop. It's the only heirloom I have from my family. The money wasn't for my business or drugs or anything else. It was for the ring. *My* ring." Feeling bold, she forged ahead, wanting him to know the whole truth. "I wanted to ask you for the money. I did. But I didn't know…"

"Didn't know what?" His penetrating gaze made her shudder.

"I didn't know…I was scared and embarrassed."

"Didn't know what, Gia?" His voice was low and rumbled with anger. She had pushed him to his limit.

Closing her eyes, she yelled out the words as fast as she could. "*I didn't know if you loved me!*" Her entire body was shaking when she finally opened her eyes back up and stared at him, waiting for a reaction.

Hart pinched the bridge of his nose and spoke calmly. "Did you see the text I sent to you?"

"Yes." Her voice was barely a whisper. "But I didn't see it until this morning. My phone was in my bag the whole time last night."

He hung his head, avoiding her stare. "Are you telling me if I had told you I loved you before you left that day, you wouldn't have gone to the club?"

"Yes." It was the truth. She was finally telling him the whole truth.

"Oh, my fucking god." He turned away and looked out the window, running his fingers across his lips in contemplation. After a few agonizing minutes of silence, he sighed again. "We're broken people, Gia. I'm broken. You're broken. We've both had our fair share of terrible mistakes." Shifting, he turned and looked directly at her, his features soft and his manner unusually calm. "I do love you."

She couldn't speak for fear of collapsing into a heaping pile of sobs. Hart was saying the words to her out loud—the words she had been so anxious to hear.

"When two broken people come together in love they can become whole again. I need you, Gia. I want to be whole. I want us to be whole."

Her lips trembled as she tried to hold back her emotions, listening to every poignant word.

"I don't care where you came from or who your mother was or what you almost went through with last night." He reached across the car interior and delicately stroked her cheek. "You make me better than I was before, and I love you. I promise I'll tell you every single fucking day from now on."

Leaning into his touch, she smiled and gazed into his deep, brown eyes, feeling the weight of a thousand pounds lifted off her shoulders. He loved her, and she was ready to be whole again too.

"I love you too, Hart," she replied sincerely. The release of those three little words off her tongue was cathartic. "And you better believe I'm going to tell you every fucking day from now on too."

He stifled a chuckle and pulled her into his arms, hugging her tightly. She relished the moment, allowing his love to finally penetrate her pores and start to put back together the broken pieces.

***

They walked hand in hand into the bedroom, the morning light appearing brighter to Hart. Immediately, he pulled off his t-shirt and watched as Gia did the same. His breathing staggered as he palmed her gorgeous breasts, making him aware of the growing bulge in his shorts. He helped ease her onto the bed and straddled her body, pulling off her yoga pants and underwear in one motion. Dragging his fingertips across her skin and circling her soft mound, he reveled in her beauty, aware that things were different now. They weren't just lovers anymore having sex. They were lovers who were making love.

"I want to indulge in every crevice, every inch of skin on your body," he whispered lustfully into her ear. Her figure hummed beneath him, the electricity between them powerful. He knew without a doubt that the love he felt for Gia was the kind of love that could destroy him.

Placing the tip of his manhood against her sweetness, he teased her playfully, making her writhe and twist with want. She moaned with pleasure, her blue eyes shining like the glint of sunlight bouncing off the surface of water. Slowly, he slid into her wet seam, taking in staggered breaths, the sensation of her tight warmth surrounding him in ecstasy. This was where he was meant to be.

She raised her hand up to his bruised cheek and stroked him, her fingers feeling like soft feathers against his skin. "I love you," she whispered.

He leaned on his elbows, positioned on either side of her dark head. "I love you too, Gia. I love you so much. I'm sorry you didn't get my message sooner…"

"Shhh," she interrupted, placing two fingers over his lips. "Fate intervened, Hart. Don't you see it? You showed up in the nick of time and stopped me from going through with something I would have regretted for the rest of my life. Your message was loud and clear."

She was right. What were the chances he and his group of friends would show up right when she was supposed to perform? It was uncanny. Fate had intervened and once again, he was grateful.

Their bodies pulsed in a slow delicious rhythm, the anticipation of climaxing building. Hart sat up, pulling her long legs up and over his shoulders, pushing himself deeper. Her moans were becoming more frequent, her nails sliding down his back, indicating she was close.

"Don't hold back," he insisted, gazing down at her beauty and watching her body pulse faster and faster. Gripping her buttocks, he could feel his release on the verge of exploding. "Oh, god, Gia. *Gia*!" They came together as one, exploding with intensity. Hart's eyes rolled back in a stupor as wave after wave hit him head-on. It was the most powerful orgasm he had ever had. Covered in sweat and trying to catch a breath, he looked at his true love who was smiling back at him. "What?" he asked, reveled by her satiation.

"You're incredible, Hart. I've never felt anything like that before."

He pulled out and collapsed next to her, bringing one of her hands to his lips and lightly placing a chaste kiss in the center of her palm. "I haven't either. It feels different when there's love involved. Does that make sense?"

She nodded, hoisting herself up, bending her elbow,

and resting her head in her hand. Running his fingers across her forehead, he gently pushed her bangs out of her eyes. "You're really beautiful, Gia."

"I am?" Her smiled made his groin pool with heat.

"Yes. You're mine." His lips made a trail of kisses down her cheek to her pink plump lips. As his tongue invaded the gap of her mouth, he could hear his sister Katie's voice calling his name.

"Hart? Hart! We're back! Surprise!"

Wide-eyed, Hart and Gia looked at each other. He wasn't expecting his sister back for another week. "Hold that thought." He bolted out of bed and grabbed his clothes from the floor. Struggling to get his feet through his shorts, he fell in haste, landing on his ass, making Gia giggle uncontrollably. Back on his feet, he quickly grabbed her by the cheeks and gave her a hard, breathless kiss. "I'll be right back."

GEORGIA ON MY MIND

CHAPTER TWENTY-THREE

"Baby girl!" Hart shouted, opening his arms wide to receive a bear hug from his sister Katie.

"Big brother!" she squealed, embracing him tightly. When she pulled back, her face radiated pure joy. "I missed you!"

"I missed you too. Where's Clay?" Draping his arm across her shoulders, they walked into the family room.

"He's getting our bags out of the car." Her brow suddenly creased with concern. "What happened to your face?"

Hart brought his hand up to his bruised cheek and chuckled. "Nothing. I was at a club with Mitch celebrating his bachelor party with the gang last night and ended up on the wrong end of some bouncer's fist. It doesn't hurt."

Stopping in the middle of the room, she stomped her foot and put her hands on her hips. "Hartford Parker! When are you going to learn you're not a teenager anymore? A barroom brawl? I thought you were past this kind of behavior and a grown up by now…"

"He was protecting my honor," Gia interrupted, standing in the doorway of the kitchen, startling Katie. She approached, extending her hand. "Hi. I'm Gia."

Katie looked at Hart with wide eyes and smiled before turning back to Gia and enthusiastically grabbing her hand. "Hi, Gia. I'm Katie, Hart's sister. It's so nice to meet you finally!" The two girls grinned and giggled, shaking hands longer than usual.

Hart playfully put his arms around both girls and sighed contentedly. "My two favorite girls in the whole wide world. I'm a happy man!"

"Hey! What's going on in here?" Katie's boyfriend Clay Watkins trudged through the hallway, his cowboy boots clomping on the floor as he carried two large duffel bags and a guitar case.

"Clay!" Hart swooped in and bear-hugged him, making him drop the bags with a thud. The two guys slapped each other on the back, Hart playfully flicking Clay's longer hair, telling him to get a haircut. After introducing him to Gia, the two couples collapsed on the couch to catch up.

"Sorry, we didn't call to let you know we were coming back early. But we wanted to surprise you."

"Yeah, man. The tour bus got back to Nashville yesterday. After a good night's sleep at my place, Miss Katie here wanted to hit the road as soon as possible to get back to Atlanta."

"Why the rush?" Hart asked, curious as to why Katie and Clay were grinning from ear to ear. Gia was snuggled next to him on the couch, intently taking it all in.

"To tell you our news… *We're engaged!*" Katie squealed with delight, holding her splayed hand out to them, showing off a huge diamond ring.

Sitting proudly next to her, Clay beamed with love, one booted ankle resting on one knee. "She couldn't wait to tell you."

"Oh my god!" Shock didn't begin to describe Hart's emotions. "Congratulations!" They were all on their feet, excited by the news. Gia was holding Katie's fingertips, admiring the ring, and Hart shook his head, tears of joy tickling the corners of his eyes. Hugging Clay tightly, he joked, "You better take damn good care of my baby girl, or I'll come after you!"

"Oh, you know I will. I love her, man. She's the love of my life!"

For the next hour, they sat around sipping on champagne Hart had conveniently kept in the fridge, celebrating the engagement of his sister to country music star, Clay Watkins. When Gia asked for details regarding the actual proposal, Katie blushed, squeezing her fiancé's knee. "I'll let Clay tell you," she said.

Clay chugged what was left in his glass and set it on the coffee table. "Here's the thing. I knew I wanted to ask her, but I didn't want it to happen on some cramped tour bus while flying down the highway and I certainly didn't want to do it on stage in front of thousands of people." He shifted, leaning his elbows on his knees, running his palms back and forth. "We had some time off while we were on the West Coast leg of the tour. There's a particular stretch of the Pacific Coast Highway I'm fond of near Malibu where the coastline has these incredible sea stacks and small caves that glow when the sun is setting."

Hart noticed his sister staring dreamily at Clay, rubbing one hand up and down his back. To see her happy and relaxed meant the world to him. It was a far cry from her days as a big-wig in corporate America when she was married to her job. He clutched Gia's free hand in his lap while listening and trying not to grin too broadly the entire time.

"I packed us a picnic and some wine from Napa we'd picked up earlier in the week and rented a car. Asked her on a real date. We parked on the bluff and took a trail down to the beach. You should have seen her. She was so excited to dip her toes in the Pacific Ocean for the very first time." They all chuckled as Clay turned to gaze at his future bride. "You finish, pretty girl."

Katie blushed as Clay sat up and put his arm around her. "The water was so cold, and I was fixated on the pools of sea-life collecting on the beach. There were so many different colored shells and wildlife. I'd never seen anything like it before, and I was oblivious to what Clay was up to. The sky was the perfect swirl of orange and pinks. It was breathtaking." She swooned, retelling the story.

"My sister's a sunset fanatic," Hart said jokingly to Gia, making them all laugh.

"When I looked up to show him one of the shells I found, he was standing next to our picnic blanket in his bare feet, leaning on a large stick. I remember his hair was blowing in the wind and his face was gorgeous in the light. He had written something in the sand, and when I figured out what it was, I started to cry."

"What was written in the sand?" Gia asked, her voice laced with anticipation.

Katie looked up at her beau with sparkling eyes. "It said, 'Marry Me.' Of course, I said yes!"

The group erupted in joyful laughter, and Hart watched as Clay leaned in and kissed his sister tenderly on the lips. They mouthed the words, "I love you" to each other, which sent a pang of happiness to his heart.

Refilling everyone's glass with more bubbly, Hart lifted his glass in a toast. "Well, here's to true love and to those who find it. Congratulations!" Watching Gia take a tiny sip of champagne, she seemed enraptured by the way he and his sister bantered back and forth; their sibling love obvious. He watched her glance at the clock over the mantel, gasp and jump to her feet. "Oh, shit! You have classes," he remembered, standing quickly. He took the glass out of her hands and squeezed her shoulder.

She offered an apologetic smile to Katie and Clay. "It was wonderful meeting you both. I'll be back before dinner."

"Good to meet you too," they said in unison, watching her run down the hall to the stairs.

Katie turned to him. "Wow, Hart. She *is* real!"

"Well, what did you think, that I made her up?" He chuckled before downing Gia's glass and setting it on the table. "She's living with me. Here. I hope that's okay. I was gonna tell you before you came home, but you kind of surprised us today." He watched her eyebrows rise with astonishment.

"She's *living* with you? Does that mean it's serious?"

Running his hands through his hair, he couldn't help the bashful smile that played upon his lips. "I love her, Katie. I want her to be with me."

Clay and Katie looked at each other in shock before looking back at him. "My big brother's in love!" she whispered excitedly. "Do Mom and Dad know?"

Hart's expression paled. "No. Not yet. They've met her, though. Several weeks ago at the club. Dad was *not* on his best behavior."

"Oh, no. Have you talked to him since?"

"Nope. Just Mom. That's okay. I don't miss him."

Clay set his glass down and looked at Hart sadly. "Dude, I hope you don't mind me saying this, but you only get one father. I know your relationship hasn't been the best recently, but you should try to make amends. I'd give anything to have my daddy back for just one more day. I don't want you to have any regrets, man."

Katie sat on the edge of the couch. "Clay's right, Hart. Make amends. Your life is on such a better track now. And you have Gia. I can see the change in you. Maybe he will too." Clay nodded in agreement.

"I don't know…"

The thought of being in the same room with his father again made Hart uneasy. Sure, he still loved him, but he wasn't about to continue to take the demoralizing bullshit he dished out. Perhaps he might see he was a changed man like his sister did. Gia was responsible for that. "Maybe," he muttered, chugging the remnants of his glass.

"Well, I already told Mom we were coming back to town earlier than expected. She wants to have us all over for dinner tomorrow night. Gia is included, of course."

How could he let down his sister who was basking in the glow of being newly engaged? It was a happy time for their family, for himself too. He and Gia were finally blatantly honest with one another, and she was done with that low-life, Bartelli and the stress of her failing business. No more entertainment gigs and no more living out of her studio. They had so much to look forward to—together. She deserved a loving family, and he had one to offer, even if his relationship with his father was at times, dysfunctional. Poor Gia never even knew who her father was. Welcoming her into their family was the right thing to do.

"Alright, alright. We're both off tomorrow. We'll come if it will make the bride-to-be happy."

Katie catapulted herself into her brother's arms. "Yay! Thank you!"

Gia reentered the room with a large bag over her shoulder, dressed in casual Capri pants and a black leotard. Hart noticed right away she had put on makeup, looking refreshed after the long night and morning. It had to be hard for her to go back to work, knowing she was closing up her business in a couple of weeks. He went to her, pulling her affectionately to his side. "You got everything you need?" he asked sweetly, aware his sister and Clay were watching them.

"Yes. I'll be back in a few hours."

Hart kissed her on the cheek. "I'm gonna walk you out."

"See ya tonight, Gia," Clay shouted.

"Yes, see you tonight!" Katie exclaimed.

When they were outside by Gia's car, Hart pushed her gently up against the driver's side door and used his fingers as a comb through the side of her hair. "I'm gonna miss you."

Her blue eyes slightly misted as she stared into his face. "I'm gonna miss you too. We still have a lot to talk about."

Hart nodded in agreement. "I know. I want to go back to that pawn shop and get your ring back."

"Hart…"

"No, Gia. I won't take no for an answer. It's something I feel very strongly about." He kissed her forehead.

"Okay," she whispered.

"Okay? You're not gonna argue with me or go sell a kidney or something crazy to get the money?" His teasing made her giggle.

"No. I'm not going to argue. I'll have to come with you though. The owner gave me until the end of business on Monday." Nodding, he looked down at her and brushed his fingertips across her cheek. "I love you, Hart. I'll do whatever you want."

His eyebrow arched and he cocked his head. "Anything I want? Now that, sweetheart, could be very interesting."

GEORGIA ON MY MIND

CHAPTER TWENTY- FOUR

The familiar click of the key in the studio door made Gia pause. A sense of relief washed over her, and she welcomed it. Things had changed and this wasn't her residence anymore. Nor was it her business for much longer. Her footsteps echoed in the expansive space as she crossed the length of the room to the corner while inhaling the familiar musty smell of the room. Setting her bag on a chair, she pulled off her pants and wrapped a black rehearsal skirt around her waist. Quickly, she put on her ballet slippers and trotted to the sound system. With the touch of her fingertip, the board came to life, the knobs glowing in red and green. Surveying the meager CD collection, she found what she was looking for and popped it into the player, jacking the volume to a hefty level. She was going old school ballet today, choosing Tchaikovsky's, *Swan Lake*.

Trotting to the middle of the room, she posed and inhaled a deep, cleansing breath, waiting for the music to start. Her reflection was graceful, her body lithe. As the melody floated throughout the space, she warmed up, closing her eyes and concentrating on the bending and flexing of her muscles. The grace and beauty of her movements ignited her passion for dance. Ballet had always been her safety net. As a young child in her aunt's studio, it was her ultimate escape from the harsh reality that was her life. As a young woman, it still brought her much comfort. She needed to find her center again, and she knew just how to do it.

Starting off with fluid spring-like pliés, she moved effortlessly, stretching her ankles and knees with pointed toes. As the music became more dramatic, she concentrated on the beautifully slow and sustained grace of the adagio. The calming effects of ballet were instant, and she felt at peace, the classical music swirling around her. As she whirled and spun in several consecutive pirouettes that would have made any audience member gasp out loud, she was vaguely aware of Ethan entering the room. When she slowed down, he clapped, the noise startling her.

"Bravo, prima ballerina! Bravo!" He stood and crossed the room to the stereo, turning the loud volume down. He skipped happily toward her, looking like he was skating across the floor in his Converse tennis shoes.

Gia blushed with discomfort. This wasn't the first time he had caught her in the act of playing out her ballerina fantasy. She approached him shyly, kissing both of his cheeks. "I'm just warming up for class."

"Warming up, my ass!"

She sat and pulled a small towel out of her bag, wiping her brow. "What?"

Ethan sat next to her. "Seriously, I have a proposition for you. Now that you're closing the studio and you'll have the time, you can't say no."

"What is it?" Drinking greedily from a water bottle, she eyed him curiously.

"I need a lead ballet dancer in the musical I'm choreographing at the City Springs Theatre."

She swallowed and held the bottle in her lap. "What do you mean? You cast that show weeks ago."

A slow, sly smile spread across his face. "Yep. But the ballerina we cast to do the dream sequence just got offered a Broadway show in New York. She leaves before opening. That means, today is your lucky day."

All of the blood drained from Gia's face, and she held her breath. "Are you kidding me? You want…me?"

"Fuck, yeah! The show opens in less than two weeks. You're the only classically trained ballerina I know in Atlanta that could pull this off and save the day!" Placing his warm palm on her thigh, he eagerly continued, "Come on, Gia. This will finally be your chance for a fresh start. A new audience will finally be able to witness what I've seen all these years—your incredible talent!"

She hesitated, not sure if she could learn a routine in two weeks. "I don't know. It sounds like a lot of work."

Grabbing her hands, he held them tight. "It will be a lot of work. But we have this entire room to practice in until you close and I'll be there every step of the way. I would never put you out on stage feeling uncomfortable or exposed."

Gia swallowed a lump in her throat. That's exactly how she felt last night at the club—uncomfortable and exposed. She never wanted to feel that way ever again.

"Don't I have to be equity or something? The only performance I have on my resume is from a couple of local recitals and my brief stint on *So You Think You Can Dance*. It's mostly teaching experience here at the studio and at some of the dance conferences that have come through town."

"Do you trust me?"

She nodded, holding her breath.

"Okay. We start on Monday. That will give me time to get everything together and let the production team know we won't have to change the choreography to that part of the show for a chorus girl. I can't wait to tell them I found a real ballerina." He popped up from the chair with enthusiasm. "It's your time, Gia! This is gonna be *awesome*!"

***

Hart and Katie lounged on the L-shaped sofa, catching up while Clay took a much-needed catnap.

"Tell me how you met," Katie requested, her brown eyes sparkling.

Hart rolled his eyes, knowing his little sister was going to press him for details until he came clean. "Well, she did this Marilyn Monroe tribute act at a party."

Her eyes became wide, and she started to giggle. "No way!"

He chuckled. "Way. I'm not making this up. She sang *Happy Birthday* to Mitch Montgomery at his birthday gathering at the club in a full Marilyn getup a couple of months ago. The whole act was professional, and she did such a great job. You know, she's a dancer. She has her own studio on the south side."

"That's cool! She teaches?"

"Yep. But Gia's studio is closing at the end of the month. The area is rundown and crime-ridden. She's lost a lot of students too. That's why she's been doing these Marilyn gigs, to supplement her lost income."

Katie's brow furrowed in concern. "I'm sorry to hear that."

"We went and grabbed coffee after Mitch's party. Things kind of took off after that first night."

"Wow. So, what's she gonna do now that her studio is closing?"

Hart dragged his hand down his stubbly face. "Well, there's a lot to do when you close up shop. That will keep her busy for a few weeks. And then there's the moving-in-together piece—"

"Yes! How did that happen?" she interrupted.

There was a part of him that wanted to tell her every detail about Gia, but also a part of him that wanted to protect her and her privacy. He decided to keep it simple and tell her the truth.

"We love each other, and we want to be together. It's

time for me to find my own place anyway. I can't be living with my little sister for the rest of my life." He playfully poked her in the arm, making her laugh. "I thought it made sense to ask her to look for a new place with me. You know, so that we could be together full time."

Katie shook her head. "Never in a million years did I ever think you would find 'the one.' I'm so happy for you!"

The back of Hart's neck grew hot. "Thanks, baby girl. I'm so happy for you and Clay too. We both have a lot to be thankful for."

"That's for sure. What's Gia's family like? Have you met them?" The question caught him off guard, making him frown. He watched Katie's expression pale. "What, Hart? Are they awful?"

He ran his tongue across his top lip, trying to figure out a way to explain Gia's horrible upbringing. "I'm not sure if this is something she would want me talking about. Her childhood was pretty traumatic."

Katie brought her hand up to her mouth with genuine concern. "Why? What happened?"

Hart shook his head and looked at his hands gripping his thighs. "There's no other way to say it…her mother was a stripper, Katie. She died of a drug overdose when Gia was nine years old. She never knew her father." When his eyes met his sister's, he noticed her shocked expression. "I shouldn't have told you that…"

"No, no. I'm glad you did. I had no idea. Poor Gia. I'm sure dancing has been an escape for her."

Nodding in agreement, Hart sighed. "It was her late aunt's studio and a safe place when she was a child. Her aunt got custody of her when her mother died. It was left to her in the will when her aunt died."

"Wow," Katie repeated, mulling over this information. "Makes you grateful for our committed parents and how we were raised, doesn't it? I mean, even if you and Dad don't get along all the time, aren't you thankful for how we grew up?"

Snapshots immediately filled his mind of him and his sister's idyllic childhood, growing up in the country club subdivision. He couldn't recall ever going without anything he ever wanted. Sure, his mom and dad made him work for the frivolous stuff like the latest cell phone or designer tennis shoes. But for the most part, he was a spoiled rich kid saturated with unconditional love, living the high life without a care in the world. Guilt washed over him as he thought of Gia and her heinous childhood. "Yes, Katie. I'm very thankful."

Grinning, she started to gather the remnants of their earlier champagne toast. "For what it's worth, maybe you can be that knight-in-shining-armor and show her a life she could have only dreamed of." She paused, holding flutes in her dainty hands. "She's a lucky girl to have met the Hart of Dixie, that's for sure."

Hart watched his sister walk away into the galley kitchen. Sighing heavily, he thought about her comment about showing Gia a life she could have only dreamed of. As he lounged dreamily on the sofa, he felt his phone buzz in his pocket and reached for it, hoping it was Gia checking in.

Dude, how are you? How's Gia?

It was a text message from his buddy, Mitch Montgomery. Images from the previous night instantly flooded his mind. How was he going to explain everything to his buddies? How were they going to react the next time they saw him with Gia? His hand trembled, texting a simple message back to his friend.

Everything good. Talk later.

Shoving the phone back in his pocket, he hoisted himself up. Katie was always the first person he talked to when something was heavy on his heart. Admittedly, he had pushed what had happened the previous night into the farthest crevice of his mind, not wanting to deal with the situation fully. But it was only a matter of time before it would rear its ugly head, causing a sort of post-traumatic-stress with flashbacks of what he had witnessed. The worst part was the "what if." What if he hadn't been there to stop her from going through with her performance? What if the entire audience had seen her naked and exposed in the spotlight? What if she were predestined to follow in her mother's footsteps and make a career out of stripping in clubs?

"Hey," he said softly, leaning his butt on the countertop and watching Katie hand-wash the champagne flutes.

"Hey," she smiled back, oblivious to the turmoil that swirled in his head.

"So…about last night."

She eyed him and pursed her lips in disappointment. "I get it that you were out clubbing with your buddies, Hart. I'm sure Clay is gonna have his own bachelor party at some point before we get married." Drying her hands on a checkered towel, she turned toward him. "But can't you keep your anger in check? Why did you get into it with a bouncer? Were you totally shit-faced?"

Looking at the floor in shame, he shook his head. He hated it that his sister assumed he was drunk. But why wouldn't she? For the first few months after his embarrassing indiscretion in DC, he stayed inebriated most of that time. "The place we were at. It was a strip club."

Her brow furrowed before her expression softened with what looked like recognition. "Oh, geez. You feel guilty for being there, and Gia doesn't know yet, huh?"

"No. Gia…" Hart swallowed a lump in his throat the size of a Georgia peach trying to gather the courage to tell her. "Katie, Gia was one of the strippers last night."

GEORGIA ON MY MIND

CHAPTER TWENTY-FIVE

Speckled light filtering through mature trees flitted in and out of the car window, making Gia squint and rummage in her purse for her sunglasses. It was a glorious day, and she was feeling better than ever. Thankfully, her last gig was behind her, and it was one she had booked herself. She was supposed to go through Franko's business when she got a referral but had decided to skip that piece and go behind his back, booking the job on her own. It was an easy gig—an eighties-themed birthday party. Dressed in her outrageous Madonna costume, she was happy to entertain guests, showing them dance moves from the era that included the Moonwalk, the MC Hammer Dance, the Sprinkler and the Running Man. The best part of the night was no strip-tease, just dancing. She was a huge hit and her tip at the end of the night proved it. Glad to have these gigs behind her, she was more than ready to turn the page.

Clay and Katie were cozy in the backseat of Hart's Mercedes as they drove through the suburbs together toward the Parker's childhood home. Katie humored them with stories about life on the road during Clay's first tour. Hart had told Gia early in their relationship his sister was dating a guy in the country music business. What he didn't tell her was how famous the guy was. Gia looked him up online, shocked to learn Clay was a Grammy-award-winning songwriter and had only recently crossed over as a touring artist, no doubt his hit songs bringing in great bank. What a coincidence he had been dubbed "Georgia Clay" by his fans. She was a "Georgia" too.

As they pulled into the driveway of the Parker home, Gia marveled at the place where Hart and his sister grew up. The large, two-story structure looked like something out of a movie, the pretty black shutters against the pristine white siding perfect in every way. Beautiful rose bushes in a rainbow of colors edged the cobbled walkway that led up to the red front door. Before Katie could grasp the knob to turn it, Mr. and Mrs. Parker threw the door open wide, energetically ushering them in. She couldn't help but watch the way Hart cautiously greeted his father, the two men awkwardly shaking hands in the foyer. Offering a polite handshake herself, Mrs. Parker saved the day by slipping her arm through Gia's, pulling her into the great room that looked out onto a massive patio and kidney-bean shaped pool. The sun shimmered on top of the water, the entire backyard area beckoning everyone to hang outside.

Gia turned to Hart's mother and presented her with a plate of homemade brownies she had made that morning. "Hope you like chocolate," she said shyly.

"Oh, yes. These will be perfect with the homemade vanilla ice-cream later."

The home was a buzz of conversation, the guys grabbing bottled beers out of the massive refrigerator while the women set out appetizers on the middle island. Katie squished her nose and shook her head, passing on the beer, opening up a large cupboard above the oven filled with several bottles of liquor. She pulled out a green bottle of English gin. "Would you rather have a gin and tonic?" she asked Gia.

"Sure." While Katie made their cocktails, Gia looked around Hart's childhood home. Everything was lovely and comfortable, from the overstuffed seating and throw pillows to the knick-knacks, and framed pictures of family spread throughout. She approached a side table and smiled as she looked down at a picture of Hart posing in his Lakeside High School football uniform. His young features were soft, but his expression was hard as if trying to convince the photographer he was a bad-ass.

"That's Hart's senior football picture. You should have seen him back in the day. Such fun times watching him from the stands." Mrs. Parker's smile was nostalgic as she stared back at the photo of her son.

"Well, I've seen that expression plenty of times. He can be so serious." Gia giggled, making a mock-frown of her own.

"Who's serious?" Hart came between the two women and draped his arms around them.

"You were, son. So serious about your football." His mom tickled his ribs, making him buck.

"Hey. We had to be serious about winning."

"Did you?" Gia teased.

He took a large swig of beer and winked back at her. "Sure did. Won the division championship that year."

With cocktails in hand, the group dispersed to the outdoor patio, the early summer day exceptionally bright. Shaded by a large umbrella table, Mr. Parker apologized that the pool wasn't quite ready for swimmers. "It was recently shocked, and now we're just waiting for these warmer days to heat the water up. The next time you're here, it will be good and ready."

"Dad never bought a heater for the pool, no matter how much I begged as a teenager," Katie explained to Gia and Clay. "That never stopped Hart. He'd jump in any time of year, especially if you offered him something he wanted."

"Like what?" Clay laughed.

"Oh, I don't know. Like the last cookie or a beer. He didn't care if his nuts shriveled up into peas."

"Katie Parker!" her mother chastised. The whole group burst out laughing except for Mr. Parker who shook his head.

"It's true. I was fearless and would do anything on a dare," Hart interjected.

"Hmmph." Mr. Parker scowled in disgust, bringing a beer bottle up to his lips. Gia couldn't help but notice Mrs. Parker shake her head slightly while patting his knee.

Clay cleared his throat and looked at Mr. Parker expectantly. The older man nodded his head and smiled. "Mrs. Parker. Your daughter has some news for you."

"Oh?"

Katie turned to her mother and grasped her hands in her own. The look of happiness that crossed her face sent a pang of want to Gia's heart. "Mom, I made Dad promise he wouldn't tell you."

"Tell me what, honey?" she asked nervously.

"Clay asked Daddy for my hand in marriage. We're engaged!"

Gia watched Katie thrust herself into her mother's open arms and wondered what it would be like to have a parent to tell news like that to. She would never know. She had been orphaned way before her own mother had died, fending for herself just trying to survive. Being around this all-American family in their immaculate house, celebrating a perfect engagement brought it all to the forefront. Would she ever experience this kind of happiness in her life? Was it in the cards for her? Was Hart really "the one"? Sliding her hand under her nose, she sniffled, aware that her emotions were dangerously close to surfacing, watching the Parker family congratulate the happy couple with hugs and laughter. She felt Hart's lips press against her temple.

"Overwhelming, isn't it?"

Could he read her mind? She exhaled and offered him a small smile before bringing her drink up to her lips and taking a large swig.

"You want to go?" he whispered in her ear, his warm breath comforting.

She closed her eyes and leaned her shaking head against his. "No. I'm fine."

"Okay. They'll settle down soon. Come help me get the grill ready." Hart stood and extended his hand helping her up.

*

"Where's your bathroom?" she asked.

"Down the hall to the left. You can't miss it." He kissed her cheek, watching her go back in the house. This was the first time she had been around his family, which made him nervous. What did she think? He could tell she was melancholy being here. But why? Was it because she never had what he did growing up? Was it because his sister and Clay were unintentionally flaunting their love and happiness after what he and Gia had just gone through? They hadn't had a whole lot of time to sit down and talk about everything. He was hoping to later that evening, away from his family.

"I meant to tell you earlier when we were alone, Gia's great." Clay stood next to the refrigerator as Hart helped himself to another beer.

"Thanks, man. She's pretty cool."

Clay looked around the room as if to make sure they were alone. "Katie kind of filled me in on everything this morning. Are you sure you two are alright after what went down the other night?"

Every muscle in Hart's body tensed. He knew his sister would tell Clay everything—she told him she would. Again, thoughts of the night at the strip-club came barreling back to the forefront of his mind. "I'm fine, Clay. No worries. We'll get through it." His tone was terse.

Clay nodded and reached out to squeeze his arm. "Okay. If you ever need to talk, I'm here for you."

When Gia came back from the bathroom, she seemed

cheerful and more talkative while he prepared the grill. At one point, she was chatting away about a class she used to teach for engaged couples wanting to learn the first dance for their nuptials.

"Hey! That's a great idea!" Katie exclaimed. She turned to Clay and batted her eyelashes at him. "We could have Gia help us come up with something really special for our wedding."

"I'd be happy to help," she offered.

Hart couldn't help but notice his father grimace.

As the sun started to dip behind the tree line of the Parker residence, they dined alfresco on grilled burgers, salad, and deviled eggs. Mrs. Parker was giddy, serving homemade ice-cream from a tall silver canister into pretty crystal dessert bowls, adding a big chunk of Gia's homemade brownies on top. The flavors of the meal and dessert reminded Hart of countless lazy summer days he had spent at his childhood home. The nostalgia was sweet as he remembered those happy days of his youth, but something was gnawing at him. Something was off. Clearing some of the plates, he made his way into the kitchen and noticed his father following him from behind.

"Son, I've wanted to talk to you all day."

Hart slid the dirty dishes into the sink and sighed. "What is it, Dad? Am I not acting a certain way? Am I embarrassing you in front of Mom?"

Mr. Parker had his hands on his hips and shook his head, a menacing smile creeping across his face. "You think you're something else, don't you? Bringing a pretty little thing like Gia into our home?"

Hart frowned hearing his father call Gia, a "thing." He used the term of endearment, "sweet thing" all the time around Gia, but hearing the word come out of his father's mouth without the "sweet" was unsettling. "What does that mean?"

He watched his dad puff out his chest. "I played a few holes of golf earlier today at the club before you all got here. Ran into a couple of your buddies on the course."

"So? You run into them all the time. That's nothing new."

"But the story they told me." He raised an eyebrow. "That *was* new. It seems your little pop tart likes to take her clothes off at a certain strip club in town."

All of the blood drained from Hart's face. This couldn't be happening. Surely his friends wouldn't have told his father what happened the other night, especially when he begged them not to tell *anyone*. It was a complete misunderstanding. Gia was *not* a stripper in the club. Leaning closely into his father's face, he spoke through gritted teeth. "You have no idea what you're talking about."

Mr. Parker jutted his chin out defiantly. "You've really made a mess of your life now, boy. Everyone is talking about it. Do you know how embarrassing this is going to be when your mother finds out? And what about your poor little sister and Clay now that they're engaged? Do you want this information leaked to the tabloids while they're planning a wedding? You know how famous he is."

Hart's hands fisted against his rigid sides.

"Get that tramp out of my house. She's not welcome here, and neither are you as long as you're dating her…"

A small gasp was heard in the hallway. Their heads whipped around to see Gia standing near the bathroom, her face deathly pale and full of remorse. Obviously, she had overheard their conversation.

"*Gia*," Hart croaked.

GEORGIA ON MY MIND

CHAPTER TWENTY-SIX

Gia moved as fast as she could to get out of there, the label "tramp" echoing in her ears. When the front door knob wouldn't turn, she could feel the panic quicken in her chest, the sound of her own heart pounding in her ringing ears. Her mother was the tramp, her years of stripping and drugs eventually killing her. She was *nothing* like her late mother. How could Mr. Parker judge her like that?

"*Gia*!" Hart wrapped his strong arms around her, pinning her against the door as she flailed. "Gia, no! Don't listen to him. He doesn't know what happened!"

Beating her fists against his rock-hard abs, she knew she was no match for his strength and eventually gave up in his arms. "Get me out of here," she begged, hiding her face in his shirt. The door opened, and they stumbled out onto the front porch, Hart practically carrying her to the car. When she was finally inside the vehicle, through hazy tears, she watched him fumble for his phone.

"What are you doing?"

"I need to text my sister and tell her to find a ride. Don't worry. I told her everything. Maybe she can talk some sense into our stupid father." He hunched over the phone, his normally perfectly combed hair tousled from the episode. Movement caught her eye out of her peripheral vision, and she turned her head to look out the window. Mrs. Parker, Katie, and Clay had come out on the front porch. She tensed in terror, not ready to confront them.

"Please, Hart. Get me out of here. *Please!*"

In a split second, he revved the car and peeled out of the driveway, the image of Mrs. Parker with her hand splayed across her chest something she would never forget. Hart gripped the steering wheel, looking anxiously over at her. "Don't let what my father said ruin everything, Gia. He always does that. He assumes the worst and makes life a living hell. Don't listen to him!"

Gia couldn't bring herself to say anything. She wanted to get as far away from the happy, shiny country-club family as she could. There was no chance in hell she would ever be welcome like Clay Watkins. He was lucky—and a successful, Grammy-award-winning, super-rich, country music star. And what was she? A broke dance teacher. A Marilyn Monroe and Madonna impersonator. A ballerina wanna-be. A homeless orphan. A *tramp*, according to Hart's father.

They drove in silence the rest of the way, Gia mulling over her next move. She needed space—time away from everyone and everything that had happened. Life was happening so fast, and she was losing her grip on her new reality. But where could she go? Angel had always said she was welcome, but she was living with her boyfriend. Imposing on them was something she didn't want to do. Her friend Ethan might be an answer. They had a lot of work to do with the upcoming opening of the show at the City Springs Theatre. Maybe he could take her in. She could always stay in the storage closet at her studio for the remainder of the month, but Hart would be relentless and hound her if he found out. By the time they got back to Katie's condo, Gia had made up her mind.

"Don't leave," Hart whispered, putting the car in park.

Gia couldn't face him. "I need some time to think, Hart. Everything suddenly got very complicated."

"No, it didn't!" He stretched his arm across the interior of the car and grabbed her hand. "We're the same two broken people who need each other, now more than ever before."

Gia closed her eyes, the brokenness consuming her.

"Please, give us a chance. Don't listen to my dad or anyone else. Listen to me. I love you. Doesn't that mean anything?"

A wave of exhaustion washed over her as she tried to be strong. "Just give me some time, Hart. That's all I'm asking. If you truly love me, you'll back off." When she turned to look at him, her breath caught at the sight of his expression. He looked so sad. She was on an emotional roller coaster and had to get off before she jumped. "I'll get my things."

***

Hart lay in the double bed, taking a long pull from the whiskey bottle. He couldn't help but inhale the scent of the pillow he held in his arms over and over, Gia's essence comforting him in his state of shock.

She was gone.

He watched in horror as she quickly packed up her belongings and loaded them into her car. When he tried to approach her with a goodbye hug, she stopped him with her open palm in front of her body.

"I can't right now," she whispered, barely making eye contact. It took everything in his power not to get on his knees and beg her to stay.

"When will I see you again?" he asked in one last attempt to communicate before she drove off.

"I don't know. I'm going to be busy with the show. Maybe after opening? I'll be in touch."

"That's almost two weeks from now. Are you kidding me?" The severity of the situation was becoming apparent.

"I don't know, Hart. Just… just wait for me to get in

touch with you. I need time."

Watching her car drive away, all he could feel was the familiar rage creeping into his bones. As much as he wanted to follow her, he didn't. There was only one escape for him—booze. Grabbing a bottle from the kitchen, he took the steps up to his room two at a time, stopping in the hallway and ramming his fist through the sheetrock.

He was sitting in the dark, the bottle between his legs when he heard a light tapping on the door.

"Hart?" The door opened, and he could see the shadowed figure of his sister in the doorframe. "Are you okay?"

He tipped the bottle up and chugged the rest before flinging it across the room, watching it shatter against the dresser.

"*Stop it, Hart!* Drinking isn't going to bring her back!" Closing the door behind her, she flicked on the lamp, making him squint in the sudden bright light.

"Go away, Katie. Just leave me be," he mumbled, his tongue feeling too big for his mouth.

"No. You need to stop! Alcohol isn't going to help. You need to know, Clay and I talked to Mom and Dad about everything. We tried to call you several times, but you wouldn't pick up. Dad knows the truth. It was a complete misunderstanding. He's very sorry, and he feels bad about upsetting Gia—"

"Oh, really?" Hart interrupted. "Fuck him. Fuck all of you judgmental mother-fuckers."

Katie sat on the edge of the bed and shook her head in despair. "You're drunk, Hart. You don't mean that."

"Oh, yes I do." He struggled to get up on the opposite side of the bed to get away from her, but when he tried to stand, he wobbled before falling forward. He attempted to brace himself as he hit the ground, one of his hands landing on a large shard of broken glass. This sent him into a rage.

"*Goddammit!*" Rocking back and forth on the floor with

his eyes clamped shut, he tried to keep his pent-up emotions in check, but it was no use. He screamed at the top of his lungs, the stress of everything pouring out in a tirade of swear words. It wasn't the pain in his palm, the deep gash bleeding profusely; it was the unbearable ache of knowing he had lost her. He had no control over anything, and she was gone.

Katie scurried out of the room, slamming the door, and leaving him alone in a pile of rubble. His face was wet with tears, his lungs burning, trying to catch his breath from screaming. How was he going to fix this? How was he going to win her back?

Leaning against the wall, he gripped his wrist and held his injured hand against his chest. The door opened again, and Clay entered.

"Let me see, man," he requested calmly, kneeling in front of him.

Hart limply shoved his bloody hand out. Clay held it in his own and started wrapping it up in a small towel he pulled out of his back pocket, trying to stop the bleeding. "You need to go wash this off. It looks deep too. We need to get you to the ER to get it checked out. You're probably going to need some stitches."

Katie re-entered the room with a broom and dustpan, not saying a word. He watched her clean up the glass, shame filling his entire being. She didn't deserve his outburst. Both of them were trying to help. Pulling his wrapped-up hand back into his chest, he eyed Clay poignantly.

"What do I do now?" The misery in his voice caused the couple to look sorrowfully at each other.

Clay put his hand on Hart's shoulder. "Just breathe, man. Things will look different tomorrow when you're rested…and sober."

.

CHAPTER TWENTY-SEVEN

Hunched over his laptop, going over the latest commission figures, Hart didn't hear the door to his office open and was startled to see a small, blonde girl peek over the top of his desk.

"Well, hello!" He sat back in his office chair and smiled. "Jennifer, am I right?"

The little girl smiled. "You remembered my name."

"I did." He stood, walked around the desk, and kneeled to be eye level with her. "What are you doing here?"

Jennifer was dressed up in a pink pinafore and white patent-leather shoes. A giant pink bow completed the outfit. Before she could tell him why she was there, two more little girls in the same exact outfit scurried in, giggling uncontrollably. Hart stood and put his hands on his hips, not sure what to make of the little girl interruption.

"Oh, god. I'm so sorry, Mr. Parker," Jessica lamented, scrambling inside after them with baby Jo-Jo on her hip. The poor woman looked frazzled.

"No, it's okay. And please, you can call me Hart at the office. We're not that formal here. Thanks for stopping in to say, 'hello.'" He grinned back at the girls. "Hello."

"Hello," they echoed, cheekily looking up at him. Julia

didn't say a word.

"Are you here visiting your daddy?" he asked, aware they were looking at his bandaged hand.

"What happened to you?" Jilly asked innocently.

Hart bit his lip and looked at his hand wrapped in a black hand-brace. He ended up needing twenty-five stitches after the horrible night he fell apart. He wasn't about to tell them the truth. "Well, I got a boo-boo and had to get a few stitches. It'll be fine in a couple of weeks."

"Does it hurt?" Jennifer asked, her little brow furrowed with concern.

"Not anymore. The doctor fixed me right up." He looked over at Jessica who offered him a tiny smile. "How are you doing?"

"Oh, you know. Surviving," she laughed nervously, shifting the baby on her hip. "Stephen's late. It's my birthday, and he asked me what I wanted. I told him I wanted a family dinner. He's so busy; we had to make it a family lunch." She nodded to herself. "Not exactly what I wanted, but we'll still manage to have fun."

Hart nodded sympathetically before looking at the girls. "Well, you all look very pretty. I'm sure your daddy is going to be very proud showing off his beautiful family."

Jessica inhaled sharply and bit her lower lip. "Let's hope so." She placed her hand on the oldest girl's shoulder. "Come on now. Let's wait for Daddy in his office." Herding the girls to the door, she spoke over her shoulder. "It was nice to see you again, Hart. Have a great weekend!"

"You do the same. Happy birthday!" The door clicked shut. Slowly, he walked back to his desk and sat in the chair, looking at his hand. It was Jessica Kaufman's birthday—and it was opening night of the musical *Oklahoma* at the City Springs Theatre. Hart had made reservations for himself the day after Gia left, hoping by now they would be reunited. No such luck.

All of his texts and phone calls the first week they were

apart were met with silence. It was hard to leave her be, but it was what she requested on that terrible night. Here it was two weeks later, and he still didn't know anything about how the show rehearsals had gone, where she was staying, or how her students were reacting to her studio closing. There was so much he didn't know, and it aggravated him. On more than one occasion he had to stop himself from going to her studio or the diner to find answers.

After his embarrassing breakdown in front of his sister and Clay, Hart promised Katie he would stop the drinking once and for all and immersed himself in work to keep his mind off things. It was the only diversion to his constant worry. That, and looking at property every night after work. The perfect condo was on a short list for him to buy, but he couldn't quite make an offer—not yet. He vowed to wait for Gia's approval, hoping she would come to her senses and move into the new space with him. He was desperate for her to love him again. Knowing he was going to see her on stage in a few hours was a relief, of sorts. She was either going to be very happy to see him or be cold and closed off, which would indicate there was no chance for a future together.

Hart sighed, leaning his head back on the seat. In a couple of hours, he'd leave the office and go straight to the theater. The wait was almost over, the dissipating throbbing of his healing hand a reminder of the chaos coming to an end. He'd have his answers tonight, but first, he was going to show his support and watch her dance in front of hundreds of people. What a stark contrast to the last time he saw her perform.

***

"Fifteen minutes," the stage manager said outside the door of Gia's dressing room.

"Thank you, fifteen," she yelled back. Because she was a "guest" performer, and a celebrity of sorts because of her stint on *So You Think You Can Dance*, Gia was given special treatment and had her own dressing room. Bouquets of colorful flowers filled the space on opening night, many from her students who were also coming to see her. She smiled, pulling a card out of an envelope tucked into a bright assortment of Shasta daisies, a gift from her friend Angel.

"*Do your thang. Love, Angel*," she read out loud, smiling broadly. Angel had been a real angel-in-disguise, helping her navigate the last two weeks without Hartford Parker by her side. She was a couch guest in Angel and her boyfriend's apartment, where she drew much-needed strength from her friend during her darkest hours. The daunting task of learning the dream ballet choreographed by her incredibly talented friend and instructor Ethan kept her mind off the continuous ache in her heart. She poured herself into the work, pushing harder and harder, wanting her Atlanta theater debut to be a success. Ethan was ecstatic with her dedication and attention to detail, allowing her to take certain liberties with the deeply emotional scenes. Several times during private rehearsals with him, she broke down, the intense drama of the story almost too realistic, mirroring her own life. She was playing the lead character, Laurey, a pretty farm girl struggling with her feelings about two men who were complete opposites. The comparison between her old life and new life was uncanny as it mirrored the musical story, and she had to remind herself she was only playing a character.

Straightening the violet bow on her long, curled wig, she looked at herself in the lighted mirror and breathed deeply, hoping Hart would be in the audience. He had texted and left a few messages the first week they were apart. When she didn't respond to any of them, they stopped altogether. She chalked it up to him being a gentleman, finally conceding to her request for time apart.

There was a light knock on the door. "Come in," she said, bringing lipstick up to her lips and applying it. She could see Ethan enter in the reflection of the mirror. "Hey! How does the house look? Anyone showing up?" she teased.

Ethan smiled and pulled up a chair to sit next to her.

"What is it?" she asked tentatively.

"I have something for you. It was delivered to the box office. I wasn't sure if I should give it to you now or afterward. I don't want it to upset you on opening night."

"What is it, Ethan? You're scaring me." She watched him pull a small velvet bag out of his suit pocket.

"There's no card, but you should know it's from Hart." He reached for her hand and tenderly placed the satchel in her palm. "I'll give you a minute."

She looked at the velvet bag and back at Ethan as he exited the room, her heart starting to pound in her chest. Pulling on the gold cord, she emptied the contents into her palm, her Aunt Caroline's ring winking at her in the light. Immediately, she slapped her hand over her mouth and held her breath. Tears of joy seeped out of the corners of her eyes.

Too embarrassed to go back to the pawn shop to let the owner know she didn't have the money to get her ring back, she had to let it go, knowing it would never be in her possession again. For Hart to have tracked the guy down and purchase the one item that meant so much to her was unbelievable. This one item had caused so much worry, grief, and angst and now, because of Hartford Parker's selfless generosity, the ring was back in her possession, filling her heart with happiness. For a brief second, she thought about texting him to thank him profusely; to tell him what it meant to her. The surge of love to her heart was exhilarating.

"Places," she heard the stage manager say. Wiping her eyes with a tissue, she smiled back at her reflection, knowing he was in the audience—she could feel him. Putting the ring into her purse, she stood and palmed the white dress that was her costume, confident and ready to make her debut.

CHAPTER TWENTY-EIGHT

Hart had spared no expense when purchasing his ticket, wanting the best view of the stage as possible. As he sat in the orchestra section of the theater, he thumbed through the glossy program and landed on Gia's bio. He had never seen her headshot before and was taken aback by her piercing blue eyes staring back at him. The colored photo must have been taken before they met because her dark hair was long and curled over her shoulders. Her smile was reserved, the entire photograph drop-dead gorgeous. The bio highlighted her time on the television show, *So You Think You Can Dance* and her many accomplishments as an award-winning dance instructor. At the end of the paragraph, she thanked her friends and students for their amazing support and for Ethan Carmichael for giving her a chance. There was no mention of him.

The lights dimmed in the auditorium, and people quickly found their way to their seats. The orchestra swelled, and the curtain opened. Hart remembered seeing the movie version of the musical, *Oklahoma*, on television when he was just a kid. His mother loved the old musicals, many of them gifted to her over the years for her own

DVD musical library. *My Fair Lady*, *Fiddler on the Roof*, and *The Sound of Music* were just a few favorites she had collected over the years. When he and his sister went in together and bought tickets to the musical touring show of *Cats* at the Fox Theatre, you would have thought she had died and gone to heaven. As the *Oklahoma* story played out in front of him, he found himself growing anxious, wondering when Gia would take the stage. Toward the end of Act One, he didn't have to wait any longer.

Gia finally entered from stage right, causing Hart to sit perfectly erect in the theater seat, holding his breath. Every cell in his being was on high alert, and he was fixated, watching her every move from the slightest bend of her supple hands and wrists to her flexing leg muscles under the flowing, white skirt. The ballet was a dream sequence, and Gia was the leading lady for the next fifteen minutes, showing the world what she had been created to do. The elaborate staging and effects were breathtakingly beautiful, the orchestral music adding to the drama. The symbolism and foreshadowing in the piece weren't lost on Hart. When the sinister character, Jud, threw her roughly over his shoulder, stealing her away from her true love, he couldn't help but tense, thinking back to that night at the seedy club, wanting to jump up on the stage and save her. The scantily clothed can-can girls reminded him of the modern-day strippers from the club—Gia standing out in her white costume, purely innocent in the scene.

She was innocent, a stark realization hitting Hart over the head like a ton of bricks. She had never belonged in that world, her beauty and talent shining brightly like the pure white costume she wore in the stunning spotlight. With Katie and Clay's help, Hart's father learned the truth after the fact and actually apologized to him, trying to make amends. Mr. Parker was adamant that he speak with Gia and apologize to her too. When he learned she had left Hart on that fateful night, he was remorseful and felt terrible guilt. It was going to take some time for Hart and his father to repair their broken relationship. Perhaps time could heal their wounds.

A very tense and engaging fight scene ensued, and Hart had to use his jacket sleeve to wipe tears from his eyes as he watched Gia anxiously crawl along the floor to her dead leading man, her dreams of a happily-ever-after shattered. Her performance was brilliant, and as the curtain closed for intermission, he was on his feet clapping as hard as he could along with the rest of the audience.

The house lights came on, and he could hear people chatting as they milled about.

"Who was that girl in the dream ballet?" He heard one woman ask.

"God, that was so intense!" Said another.

Clenching his jaw, he couldn't help the pride that blossomed in his chest. He had to see her. He had to let her know their love wasn't dead—it was just the beginning.

*

The sound of the applause was music to Gia's ears as she remained in her final, dramatic position lying across her leading man, waiting for the curtain to close. When they were in the clear, he helped her to her feet, and the entire cast rushed the stage, crowding around them. Ethan wedged his way into the circle, rewarding her with a bear hug.

"Holy shit! That was epic! How do you feel?"

She was still inhaling and exhaling, trying to come down from the exertion of her body. "Amazing," she managed to say while breathing heavily. Her part of the show was over, and she could relax until curtain call. Her castmates were gracious and complimentary as she made her way back to the dressing room, looping her arm through Ethan's. When they were behind the closed door, Ethan nodded exuberantly.

"Seriously, you killed it. Thanks for making me look so good." The two hugged affectionately. "I was worried before."

Grabbing a towel, she sat on a chair and gently dabbed the perspiration on her face. "Worried? Why?"

"You've been through a lot these past couple of weeks. I wasn't sure how you'd react getting an opening night gift from Hart."

She nodded in agreement. "I don't want you to worry anymore. I'm happier than I've ever been in my life. And you're a big reason for that."

"I am?" he asked, his eyebrow cocked with surprise.

"Yes."

He glanced at his watch and cursed under his breath. "I gotta go. See you for the curtain call!"

Gia laughed. "Okay!"

Forty-five minutes later, the entire cast bowed to a standing ovation. When Gia stepped out for her bow, she swore she could hear Hart whistling. The whole night had been a dream come true. Without a doubt, her Aunt Caroline would have been immensely proud, the years of her teaching and coaching shining through in her performance that night. She was feeling light and carefree, changing out of her costume ready to meet her friends and students in the lobby. Hopefully, Hart was waiting for her too. Several patrons congratulated her while she signed programs, her eyes searching the lobby, but there was no sign of him.

"Oh. My. God!" her friend Angel yelled across the room. She was decked out in a purple fringe dress and teetering on high heels. The sight of her dear friend made Gia's cheeks flush with excitement, and the two propelled themselves into each other's arms.

"Girl! That was incredible! Why aren't you on Broadway or dancing in music videos?" Angel was holding her by the shoulders, looking her up and down as if she didn't recognize her.

Gia laughed and shook her head. "I'm so glad you liked it. I couldn't have pulled it off without all those extra rehearsals with Ethan."

"Well, with or without his help, you are one amazing diva!"

They chatted for several minutes as other theatergoers and some of her star-struck students politely interrupted, asking for selfies and more autographs. It was such a surreal state to be in; a far cry from the last time she had performed on a stage.

"Did you see him?" Gia asked softly so only Angel could hear.

"No, I didn't. But that doesn't mean he wasn't here."

"He sent an opening night gift. My Aunt Caroline's ring."

Angel gasped before a huge smile overtook her face, exposing the gap between her two front teeth. "Well, there it is." She reached out and straightened the collar of Gia's blouse. "Now aren't you glad you packed that little overnight bag?"

"Seriously, what would I do without you?" The two friends hugged.

"I won't wait up," Angel teased, making Gia laugh out loud.

Walking back down the corridor to the side entrance to the backstage area, she felt like she was floating on air and couldn't help but do a happy pirouette.

"Gia…"

The familiar voice stopped her in her tracks, the sound of her name coming from Hart's mouth like a beautiful prayer. When she turned around, their eyes met, and he smiled warmly at her. "You were… that was…"

It touched her that he couldn't find the words and she watched him run his hand nervously through his hair. She immediately noticed a bandage covering it.

"What happened to your hand?"

He exhaled through his nose and looked at the floor. "It's nothing. A few stitches."

"Hart…" She approached him, her eyes searching his.

"I'm so sorry."

He looked at her, nodding in agreement. "I'm sorry too."

"The ring. I…I can't thank you enough."

"I promised I would get it back for you."

Staring up into his face, she was tempted to run her hand across his chiseled features, but she held back. "You sure did. Thank you."

"You're welcome."

They stood in awkward silence as one of her castmates walked by. "See you at the party!"

"Yeah, see you there." She looked at Hart again, not knowing what to say.

His shoulders slumped, and he offered a smile tinged with sadness. "Seriously, I'm very proud of you." He reached out and squeezed her shoulder, his touch sending a jolt of electricity through her body. "Have fun at your party." His eyes crinkled as he offered one last smile before he started to walk past her in defeat, which sent a bolt of anger through her.

"That's it?" Her voice was laced with irritation as she whipped her head around to watch him go. He was so standoffish and subdued. This was not the same Hartford Parker who took complete control of a situation. Perhaps she had destroyed him after all.

"Gia…" he started. When he turned around, he tilted his head, and it took every fiber of her being not to catapult herself into his arms. "I don't want to keep you if you have somewhere to be. You were amazing tonight, and you need to celebrate this milestone. I don't think it's the right time for us to hash everything out. Enjoy the moment."

Nodding, she waited for him to say more. When he didn't and started to leave again, she couldn't take it anymore. She grabbed his arm, forcing him to turn sharply. They were within inches of each other, his brown eyes soft and melancholy in the light.

"Don't leave," she whispered, her voice cracking with emotion. "I don't want you to leave."

His brow furrowed as he searched her face. Finally, he relented, pulling her into his chest. She wrapped her arms around him and held on for dear life. She didn't want to let go—not ever. He was the one.

"Do you love me?" His whisper was anxious in her ear, and she nodded aggressively. "You do?" Pulling back from her, he held her face in his hands, looking intently into her eyes. "Say it."

"I love you, Hart." She watched him close his eyes and exhale.

"Say it again."

"I love you."

He pulled her forward and peppered her cheeks and forehead with tiny kisses as she repeated the words over and over.

"I love you. I love you. I love you…"

He pulled back a final time, and she could see tears glisten in his eyes. "Oh, Hart. Don't cry."

Instead of replying, he smashed his mouth against hers, his tongue passionately prying the seam of her mouth open, his love rushing in like river rapids. He wasn't destroyed. With three little words, she had brought him back to life.

GEORGIA ON MY MIND

CHAPTER TWENTY-NINE

"Come with me to the party, as my guest," she breathily requested in his ear.

He moaned with want. "Okay. I can stay in the background while you talk shop with your cast. As long as I can watch you from a corner and admire your beauty— and your fine ass."

She giggled into his mouth, their tongues slowly egging each other on, the want in her belly burning. The night couldn't get any better. Hart was back in her life.

"I need to get my things." Pulling back, she noticed his full, moist lips shimmering in the light. He was a sight for her sore eyes, dressed to the nines in his suit and tie; the most handsome man she had ever laid eyes on. "Come with." Grabbing him by his uninjured hand, she pulled him confidently backstage. Several cast members lingered in the halls and eyed them with interest. "Last door on the left," she whispered, knowing exactly what she was about to do. Being a gentleman, he opened the door, palming it so she could walk through first.

"Thank you," she smiled, grabbing him by the tie and pulling him into the room.

"What are you doing?" He chuckled.

Quickly, she locked the door and turned around to face him while slowly unbuttoning her blouse.

"Gia...here? Now?"

She nodded while sauntering toward him, the burning in her lower region about to combust. He took off his suit jacket and loosened his tie, pulling it up and over his head. He fumbled with the buttons of his shirt with his injured hand. She tossed her blouse to the side and came to his aid, standing before him in her lacy bra, slowly unbuttoning him. As his broad chest was revealed one button at a time, she ran her fingertips lightly across his skin, making him shiver. "We don't have much time." Unbuckling his belt, she hurriedly unzipped him and brought his pants down to his ankles along with his boxers. As she started to lower herself to take him into her mouth, he grasped her head, pulling her back up.

"I need to be inside you."

Shedding her pants and bra, she turned her backside to him, gripping the edge of the makeup table in front of the lighted mirror, completely naked. His free hand ran across her bare buttocks as she spread her legs and assumed their favorite position.

"You are so fucking beautiful." He grasped her hips, and she could feel the tip of his hardness at her opening.

"Go fast and hard," she requested, keeping her eyes glued to his in the reflection. He clenched his jaw and nodded before slamming into her with purpose. It was difficult to keep quiet so her cast wouldn't hear, her fingernails digging into the wood of the table. Hart's expression was primal as he powerfully pounded her with force. Leaning on her elbows, she pushed her butt up higher, and he pulsed deeper, causing the familiar quickening inside to take over. His hand came around to her front, and he stroked her clit with his thumb, pushing her over the edge. "Oh, god, yes!" she mumbled, wanting so badly to cry out.

"I'm about to come, baby."

"Yes. Me too." With a final thrust, she was free-falling while his rigid body stopped and he trembled, pouring a surge of warmth into her. They were both heavily breathing, trying to come down from the fast, intense orgasm and their eyes met in the reflection of the mirror.

"Goddammit, I love you so much, Gia."

She laughed in between deep breaths. "I love you too, Hart. So much."

***

A jazz trio playing familiar Broadway tunes greeted guests in the magnificent Buckhead mansion of Atlanta millionaire Pete Martin. He was one of the City Springs Theatre's top billing donors, having "Director's Circle" access to the successful shows opening in the South's newest regional theater. A generous theater connoisseur, Pete was a huge fan of musicals and insisted on hosting the opening night party for the *Oklahoma* cast. Gia had warned Hart about Pete's outrageous sense of fashion, often wearing colorful over-the-top clothing that looked like costume pieces from Cirque de Soleil. She was correct. The fifty-something eccentric looked like a space cowboy, donning pink chaps over white pants and a crystal embellished button-down shirt topped off with a large diamond enhanced bolo tie as he greeted them in the foyer. His designer glasses were black and white, resembling the hide of a cow. It took Hart a minute to take it all in.

"Darling!" Pete greeted Gia with a kiss on both cheeks and grabbed her hands. "You were brilliant. Everyone is talking about you!" He changed his focus to Hart, raising an eyebrow. "And who is your handsome date this evening?"

Gia giggled, introducing Hart. "This is Hartford Parker. He's my boyfriend."

"Nice to meet you," Hart said.

Pete grabbed his hand and stroked it, a sly smile crossing his lips. "Be still my Hart. Please, come in and make yourself at home." Hart couldn't help but notice the man's hands were incredibly soft.

People crowded every room, and Hart recognized some of the cast. He wondered who the other people were and assumed they were stage crew or family members. Gia was a doting girlfriend and introduced him to everyone she knew. And everyone went on and on about her incredible performance. Gripping his hand, she often blushed at the accolades. Hart watched her with intensity, bursting with pride. She needed this. She needed to feel what it was like to be admired for her talent and not her body.

"Do you need a refill?" he asked, kissing her lightly on the cheek.

"Sure." She handed off her crystal wine glass to him. "Come right back," she teased, her blue eyes sparkling with love.

Hart smiled and politely excused his way through the crowd toward the open bar area. As he waited in the short line, he felt a tap on his shoulder. When he turned around, his face lit up at the sight of Ethan.

"Hey! Congratulations, man! What an incredible opening night." Hart leaned in for a hug, slapping Ethan on the back.

"Yeah. What a night. What did you think of our girl?"

Hart shook his head while trying to find the words. "She was breathtaking to watch. Your choreography was amazing."

"Thanks, man." Ethan looked at the floor and shuffled his feet before looking Hart in the eye. "She had a hard time, you know."

Hart swallowed, his shoulders slumping with this news. He and Gia had only reunited, and he still had so many questions about their time apart. "I'm sorry about that. It was hard for me too. I was only doing what she wanted, giving her space."

Ethan nodded. "The show kept her mind off everything, for the most part. But some of those scenes were challenging. She comes across as strong, but she's fragile, Hart. Please don't hurt her."

"Of course not."

"I'll see you later, Hart." Ethan touched his arm and smiled.

"See ya." Hart watched him disappear into the crowd.

Carefully carrying two drinks, one in his bandaged hand, Hart looked around for Gia and spotted her near the fireplace, chatting with Pete, surrounded by some of her castmates. He stayed where he was and watched her throw her head back and laugh.

Earlier in the car, she had read him a few social media posts on the City Springs Theatre website from folks who had been at opening night, including a reviewer from the *Sandy Springs Post.*

We can't say no to this musical theater evening at the City Springs!

More than OK!

Its energy and honesty still exhilarate!

The three leads were excellent!

With each review tag read, Gia became more animated and excited, the Post review causing a tear to appear in Hart's eye.

"Choreographer, Ethan Carmichael manages an homage to the dazzling ingenuity of the original choreographer, Agnes de Mille. The Out of My Dreams ballet featuring James Hood and Gia Bates dancing the roles of Curly and Laurey was a highlight. An exquisitely fluid and majestic sight to behold!"

Watching her now among her peers, Gia dipped her head in awkwardness as her surrounding friends hugged and touched her often. She was a star in their eyes—a force to be reckoned with. What did this mean for them as a couple? He knew what it meant to be a performer—Clay Watkins' life was proof of that. Clay and his sister were barely home for a week before they had to head back out on the road, promoting his latest album. Life as an artist was hard; a lifestyle choice that came with many sacrifices.

Katie had privately lamented that she sometimes wished they could settle down and live like an average couple. But she understood the decision she had made. Katie wanted to be with Clay because she loved him and couldn't imagine her life without him. His career was in country music, and she understood the sacrifices it took to stay in the game. Gia was at a crossroads, whether she knew it or not, and had a window of opportunity to do something pretty remarkable. Without the weight of a failing business holding her down anymore, she could do anything she wanted now in hotspots like New York or Los Angeles. The sky was the limit.

Watching her beautiful face beaming with happiness, he knew he could never be the one to hold her back, no matter how much in love he was with her. She had reinvented herself and was thriving. They had just reunited, and the very thought of losing her again caused his hands to tremble. He had to set her glass of wine and his soda water on a table, shoving his hands in his pockets. A wave of sadness was creeping into his being, and he didn't want to ruin the evening. His gaze wandered to a wall of windows, looking out onto a beautiful terrace. He decided to get some air.

The early summer evening was gorgeous, and so was Pete Martin's backyard. Hart leaned over the sturdy stone ledge and looked out over a small pool glowing with dramatic underwater lighting. The back lot was heavily wooded, and he noticed lighted paths along perfectly trimmed boxwoods and azalea bushes. The soothing sound of water could be heard coming from a small fountain near a gazebo in the corner, and the peeping of late-night critters gearing up for their evening symphony in the woods. The sky was clear, and the stars were bright as he tilted his back taking it all in.

"Hey, you. What are you doing out here all by yourself? You're missing out on the Alaska flambé," Gia giggled, wrapping her arms around his middle.

He rested his chin on her head and sighed from her touch. They both looked out over the beautiful yard in silence.

"Thanks for being here with me tonight. It means a lot."

Pulling back from her, his voice was gravelly as he used the pads of his thumbs to stroke her cheeks. "I wouldn't have missed it for the world." Even in the dark, her smile was radiant.

She cupped his chin with her hand and pulled him forward, kissing him lightly on the lips. He was frozen in place, intrinsically aware of even the slightest touch of her hands and lips as she worshipped his face. His eyes clamped shut, savoring the magical moment. It was just Gia and him, and he wanted it to stay that way, forever. "You have to know how proud I am of you," he exhaled.

"Thank you."

"Y'all are going to sell out this entire run."

"Hmmm," she hummed happily, squeezing him tight. "Take me home," she whispered.

It felt like home when she was with him. It didn't matter where they lived as long as they were together. Hart could handle a sold-out run. Hell, he could handle Gia Bates being a permanent dancer at the City Springs Theatre. But he was no fool. The light had shone down on her that night on stage, and as he held her under the starry sky, he knew it was only a matter of time before her career took off like a rocket.

GEORGIA ON MY MIND

CHAPTER THIRTY

It was early, the sun had just come up and the light of day seeped through the edges of the closed blinds in Hart's room. He hadn't slept much, holding Gia most of the night in his arms, feeling her breathe in slumber. Flashback images of her jumping and twirling on the stage kept coming to mind, her face full of passion and emotion. Such a stark contrast to the last time he saw her on stage. As mesmerized as he had been watching her perform, he knew she had touched others with her talent, the audience reaction proof of that. Patience had never been a virtue he could maintain, and it was messing with him again now. He wanted to know what was next. What did the future hold for him and Gia?

Before she fell asleep, she had told him the studio officially closed and she only had a few more things to pack up and load into a storage unit she had rented nearby. He felt terrible for not being there during the transition; for not being there to help her during her strenuous rehearsal schedule while closing her business at the same time. This was just another example of her extraordinary gumption and will to make it on her own.

Stirring in his arms, he looked down at her lying across

his chest, her eyes fluttering open. The smile she offered him in the soft light made his manhood stir.

"Good morning," she rumbled.

"Good morning." Using his index finger, he gently moved her hair out of her eyes. "Did you sleep okay?"

She squeezed him tightly and sighed with bliss. Nodding into his chest, she shifted, looking up into his face. "Sure beats sleeping on Angel's sofa." Her voice was laced with humor, but her comment still made him feel incredibly guilty.

"I hate that. I hated this whole time we were apart." Wanting to be honest with her, he decided to be bold and start the conversation about their future. "Where do you see this going? So much has happened in such a short amount of time. What do you want, Gia?"

"My, my. So serious already this morning," she teased while mock frowning.

Hart shifted her body off of him and sat up, clicking on the bedside lamp. "I am serious, Gia. I want to be with you. I want us to make plans for our future. What do *you* want?"

He watched her sit up and gather the sheet against her naked chest. Her face was pure, scrubbed clean from the show makeup from the night before, her expression pensive. "You know I want to be with you too. I could bring my stuff back over here and we could—"

"No," Hart interrupted. "We're not living here at my sister's condo anymore. We need a place of our own, together."

"Okay..."

With renewed energy, Hart grasped Gia's hands in his own. "I found a condo I'm ready to buy, but I wanted your approval first. We could start over, you and me, in our own place."

She was watching him with her big blue eyes and seemed to struggle for a response. "I'd love to see it, and I'd love to move in with you. But you know after the City

Springs run, I may do some auditioning and try to land a touring show or a residency somewhere." Her eyes suddenly filled with tears. "My career is changing—my goals have changed, Hart. That doesn't mean I don't love you. But I don't know where I might end up, and I don't want to let you down by promising to move in somewhere when I don't even know where my next job is going to be."

Hart understood her hesitancy. She was right. Everything was up in the air. The timing of buying a condo and planting roots as a couple in Atlanta wasn't the best idea after all.

"Then I'll wait," he replied matter-of-factly. At this point, he was willing to do anything in his power to keep Gia in his life. "As much as I want to settle down with you, Gia, I know you have to explore this next phase of your career. I'll support you in any way I can, and I'll always be there for you." He sighed, laying his head back on a pillow. "Katie and Clay still have several months of touring. She said we're welcome to stay here as long as we need. As much as I want to buy that condo, I can wait."

Her expression went from grief-stricken to joy in a heartbeat. She relaxed her shoulders and tilted her head, looking at him. "I don't know what I did to deserve someone like you."

He pulled her into his arms again and smiled, knowing full well he didn't deserve her. "That makes two of us."

***

As expected, the City Springs Theatre run of the musical *Oklahoma* sold out. Thankfully, Hart had purchased several more nights of tickets before there were none to be had. On one particular evening, he unexpectedly ran into his father and mother in the lobby of the theater after one of the shows. Even though Hart was back on speaking terms with his father, it was a tense moment at first, Mr. Parker insisting Hart bring Gia to the front of the house so he could apologize to her in person.

After some coercing, Hart looked on as his father held Gia's small hands in his own. Her jaw was clenched as she listened to him apologize while Hart's mother looked on with tears brimming her eyes.

"I'm an old fool," Mr. Parker grieved. "Your performance was breathtaking and I had no business judging you before. You are a gifted dancer and I am very pleased that you are with my son." He was obviously moved by her performance. "Please, Gia. Won't you forgive me? Won't you give me a second chance?"

Gia hesitated for a split second before she wrapped her arms around the old man's neck and hugged him. Mrs. Parker burst into happy tears and all four of them embraced as Hart and his father leaned into each other and nodded. The past was finally behind them.

Gia was thriving in her new life, basking in the real world of professional dance, far away from her days working for Bartelli's entertainment company. There were two weeks left of the show, and she was making plans to visit New York and meet with potential agents to further her career. As much as Hart wanted her to stay put in Atlanta, he had promised he would support her no matter what. The very thought of her leaving again caused a weight to settle in the pit of his stomach. It didn't help matters that his own career was suffering because of a certain, incompetent jackass for a boss.

"Knock-knock." Stephen Kaufmann rapped his knuckles on the door to Hart's office before coming in. He stood towering over the desk with his hands on his hips. "You ever gonna get that commission report done? I've asked for it twice, and accounting's been on my ass wanting it for days. What's the holdup?"

Hart looked at his boss with disgust. The commission report was Stephen's job to approve and send to accounting. With all of his extra-curricular activities of carrying on with his mistress, he dumped the responsibility onto Hart, promising to make it worth his while. The only thing he made it was miserable, the continuous badgering and the workload almost too much to tolerate. If Hart was aware of his lack of patience in the past, he should have known it was coming to an end with Stephen Kaufman.

"Well, Stephen, when you give me something two days ago that normally takes a week to complete, I'm coming up a little late, that's all."

"Okay, okay. My bad, I admit it. I should have given this to you last week, but I was a bit preoccupied with some things going on at home."

Hart suddenly became interested, knowing Stephen's home-life with his wife Jessica and four daughters was anything but ideal. "What's going on, if you don't mind me asking?"

Stephen rolled his eyes. "Jessica found out about Traci and me…"

"Oh, God." Hart knew it was only a matter of time before Stephen Kaufman's sordid little affair came crashing down around his family.

"Yep. She caught us in bed at my house. I thought Jess and the girls were staying with her parents for the weekend. Surprised the hell out of me."

"I'll bet." Hart's inner dialogue was screaming obscenities at what a fool Stephen was, images of his own past infidelity in DC flashing through his mind. The thought of Jessica and her daughters having to experience that heartache made him sick to his stomach.

"The little bitch is threatening divorce. She says she's going to take me for every penny I have. Ha! Little does she know a certain prenup she signed years ago will prevent that from ever happening. She's getting next to nothing. I'll make sure of it."

Hart had to stand, his hands fisting at his sides. "What about your daughters?"

Stephen stifled a frown. "Yeah, I'll have to shell out a pretty penny in child support, I'm sure. I never wanted that many kids in the first place, especially girls. I should have known Jessica and all her pink would damn me to a world of daughters." Hart watched as the man dared to look him in the eye and speak. "Life would sure be a hell of a lot easier without them."

Swallowing to keep the bile from reaching his mouth, Hart glared at Stephen. The Kaufman daughters were precious. Even the small amount of time he had spent with them had shown him how sweet and innocent they were; all four of them displaying unique personalities. For their own father to cast them aside as a nuisance was beyond his comprehension. The thought of any more pain brought to those little girls and Jessica was sickening. The next sentence out of his mouth surprised him. "I quit."

"Excuse me?"

Hart started to shut his laptop down and gather a few items, shoving them into his briefcase. "Yeah, you heard me. I quit. I no longer want to work for someone as slimy and conniving as you."

"What the hell?" The look on Stephen's face was almost comical. The guy didn't know what hit him.

"Do your own goddamn commission reports. And for the record, I'm letting HR know about every single time you asked me to cover for your ass, including those times you fucked your mistress on the company dime. It's over Kaufman. Have a nice life." Hart confidently strode past Stephen in a huff.

"You stupid little fucker, you're one to talk!" Stephen yelled. "I gave you a chance when no one in our industry wanted to come near you with a ten-foot pole! You think HR is gonna believe someone like you? I'll bury you! Mark my word, you'll never work in this town again!"

Hart was barely able to make it out of the office without gripping his hands around Stephen's throat and strangling the bastard. He was done.

***

"What are you doing home? You're never home this early." Gia was sitting on the sofa with her laptop on the coffee table. Papers were spread out before her, and she was holding a coffee cup. Her call time for the show wasn't until five-thirty, and they usually managed to have a quick snack together before she left.

Hart put his briefcase on the dining room table and shrugged off his suit jacket, hanging it over a chair. Loosening his tie, he collapsed next to her on the couch and placed his hand on her thigh. "What are you working on?" he asked with interest.

Her face lit up as she reached for the computer and snuggled into him. "I'm working on my website. It's a work in progress, but I've managed to import some great photos and added a bio page. I had to get permission to use some of the live shots from *So You Think You Can Dance*. As long as I don't put together a video to sell or anything like that, I'm allowed to use them. What do you think?"

Resting his chin on her shoulder, he peered at the computer screen as she scrolled through several pages of her site. Each image was stunning, capturing Gia mid-dance move, the strength, and elegance of her body breathtaking. She clicked on a video clip, and he watched as she performed a musical theater piece from *Thoroughly Modern Millie*, and another hip-hop dance with a sturdy Latino guy, both of them dressed in high-top tennis shoes and retro-graphic tee's. She had told him she made it into the top-twenty on the live show but was then cast off, which ended her season. Hart couldn't grasp why she'd been cast off because he couldn't take his eyes off her. Gia owned the stage, and he knew without a doubt she was meant to dance.

"That's so great," he managed to say.

She turned and looked at him with concern. "Is everything okay? You didn't tell me why you're home so early."

Hart nodded, shifting in his seat, and hunching over his thighs. Rubbing his palms together nervously, he admitted what he had done. "I quit my job today."

Gia waited for a beat as if soaking in the news. "What did Stephen do now?"

Hart blew a breath of air out through his nostrils. "Jessica caught him and his girlfriend in bed together. They're getting a divorce."

"Oh, no. Those poor little girls."

"I know."

"Did you lose your cool? Did anything bad happen when you told him?"

Trying to find the words was a struggle. "I just couldn't do it anymore. I couldn't live his lie." He felt Gia wrap her arms around his waist.

"You'll find something else; something better. In the meantime, you can be my full-time cabana boy."

Eyeing her with a cocked brow, he couldn't help but smile. "Cabana boy, huh? If I recall, I kick ass at that job."

"Yes, you do. I'm hiring you on the spot." Her eyes sparkled with love.

Hart closed his eyes and smiled with relief. Leaving his job might have been the best idea, after all, leaving him open to pursue something else. Real estate jobs were in every city in the country. He didn't have to sweat it out in Atlanta, being black-balled by Stephen Kaufman. He'd wait to see where Gia landed, and they could both begin their new life together; a fresh start for both of them. The broken pieces were coming together.

"Got any plans for the next hour? Your cabana boy would like to service you."

Gia stifled a smile, her hand sliding in between his thighs and stroking his growing bulge. "That would be wonderful."

FOUR MONTHS LATER

Hart sipped on an iced-latte as he peered out the window of the corner coffeehouse, the yellow taxis and throngs of people keeping his mind off his eagerness to see Gia. She was late, which was a good sign, attending a final callback for the Radio City Rockettes. They had arrived in the Big Apple several months ago and took their time getting their bearings. Hart had found an affordable loft apartment for them on the East side, and the two of them settled into their new home with excitement. Gia spent most days pounding the pavement, querying agents and auditioning. In between her appointments and auditions, she found time to attend dance classes, perfecting her craft and staying on top of her physical health.

They had an understanding—Hart would take care of everything financially while Gia concentrated on her dance career. It didn't take Hart long to land, scoring a brokerage position in a relatively new property management firm in Manhattan. His new boss had never even heard of Stephen Kaufman, only looking at the bottom line of Hart's impressive portfolio. It was an exciting time for the happy couple, their days filled with career goals and their nights consumed with passion. Hart was the ultimate cabana boy and knew without a doubt, Gia was the one. He felt whole now—complete. Gia Bates was his entire world, and he was finally at peace.

Earlier in the week, she had gone to the cattle-call audition for the Radio City Rockettes, describing the scene to him later that night while she stretched her weary limbs in a hot bath.

"You could tell all the young dancers had big dreams in their hearts by the wonderment in their expressions," she said as he sat on the edge of the tub, keeping her company. "Knowing I could be a part of a sisterhood like that is so exciting and romantic. Thank God I got a callback!"

She had been gone the entire day, waiting patiently in a long line to sign in. Once inside, she was escorted with other girls into a large studio and taught a combination. There was a quick elimination based on height, weight, look, dance ability and retention. Gia was blessed with long legs, standing tall at 5'8" and made the first cut.

"You can't go in and 'wow' the judges. They don't want you to stand out. You had to have the exact look and position as the girl right next to you. No extra personality at all. It's a lot harder than it looks."

Hart couldn't help but smile as he reminisced about the previous evening, Gia's excitement and enthusiasm contagious. Taking a sip of his coffee, he caught a glimpse of her prancing across the crosswalk, her extraordinary legs going on for days beneath the short skirt she wore. Her blue eyes hid behind large-framed sunglasses, the summer sun shimmering off her dark hair that grazed her shoulders. He stood next to the table, ready to greet her. If the news was good, he knew she'd just smile and nod her head. If the news were bad, she'd start rambling about where she went wrong and how she was going to improve for the next time. He loved that about her—how she never gave up or felt sorry for herself. Gia always found a way to see the rainbow in the storm.

Holding his breath, he watched her enter the shop and look around for him. When she spotted him, her smile was slow as it blossomed across her face. She took the sunglasses off and started toward him.

"Well?" He couldn't take it any longer. All the days of endless auditions and callbacks finally landing a chance to be a Rockette came down to this moment. Something she had dreamed of since she was a child could finally be a possibility. He wanted it for her so badly.

She began to nod her head, the infectious grin on her face making his heart palpitate. "I made it," she whispered excitedly. "I'm going to be a Radio City Rockette!"

"Oh my god!" Hart lunged at her, swinging her around the tiny space. As he set her down, he held her face in his palms, smashing his lips against hers. "I'm so proud of you, Gia. You did it!"

"*We* did it! I can't believe it—I don't think it's sunk in yet." She was looking up at him with big blue eyes, her face flushed with surprise. "They also chose me to be a media representative."

"A media representative? What's that?"

She tucked her hair behind her ear as her eyes shone with eagerness. "It's a speaking position for televised events where we perform for publicity, public appearances, and signings. I'll have to go through professional media training for it. And it brings in lots of extra income as well as recognition."

"That's incredible, baby! You're going to be so good at this."

"Hart, this is a huge feather in my dancer's hat. I'm going to be a part of a historical sisterhood." She lunged, hugging him tightly.

"This is cause for a celebration. Come on." Grabbing her by the hand, the two of them exited the coffeehouse and walked briskly toward the subway entrance. Hart couldn't help the perpetual grin plastered on his face as they were transported twenty blocks to their neighborhood, Gia eagerly chatting away, giving him every minute detail about her audition. When they were finally at the door to their apartment, Hart turned to her with a request.

"Close your eyes."

Her smile caused his breath to hitch. "Okay. If you say so." Covering her eyes with her hands, he led her through the doorway into their home. She started sniffing the air. "What is that wonderful smell? Did you clean or use a new air freshener?" she asked.

Hart chuckled and flicked on the lights. Pleased with what he had prepared earlier, he gripped her shoulders and leaned down to whisper in her ear. "Open your eyes."

Gia brought her hands down to her sides, her eyes fluttering open. An audible gasp came from her lips. While she had been away on one of the most important days of her life, he had orchestrated a slew of florists delivering several bouquets of flowers. White lilies, red, pink and white roses, purple lilacs and an assortment of colorful hydrangea spread out over the entire great room of their loft, the aroma of the flowers sweet and fragrant.

"Hart…" she started to say. "When did you…? How did you…?"

He put his hands on her shoulders and turned her to face him. "I wanted today to be special. You've worked so hard for so long. I want this to be a day you will never, ever forget."

She looked up at him with big eyes, the surprised look on her face evident. "But…"

"But what, sweetheart?"

"But…what if I didn't make it? How did you know?"

Hart shook his head and used his index finger to tuck her hair behind her ear. "I had a gut feeling and went with it. Even if you hadn't made it, I wanted you to know how special you are to me. That I love you." He watched her bite her lower lip and blink back tears. "I'm so very proud of you. I'm proud of us." Taking a deep breath, he grasped her hands in his and lowered himself to one knee.

"What are you doing, Hart?" she squeaked, watching his every move.

He kissed the top of her hand and pulled a small velvet box out of his pocket, flicking the lid open, revealing a stunning diamond ring.

"*Hart?*"

He swallowed hard, trying to keep his emotions in check. "Gia, you've shown me what true love and passion is, not only in our relationship but in your hard work and desire to be a dancer." He watched as tears began to trickle down her cheeks as she hung on his every word. "I love it that your dreams are coming true. Mine are too. Being together, in this city, making a new life together is a dream come true." Tears pricked the corners of his eyes. "I love dreaming with you while I'm wide awake." His smile beamed across his face as he took the ring out of the box and gripped it between two fingers. "Gia, will you marry me?"

She didn't hesitate, nodding excitedly. "Yes! Yes, of course, I'll marry you!"

Hart slid the ring onto her delicate hand before the two of them stared at each other in awe. Before he knew it, she had pounced on him, taking him down to the floor, kissing him hard on the mouth, surrounded by the sea of flowers. His hands slid down her backside and gripped her buttocks, his heart two sizes too big for his chest. He had never imagined such happiness before. He was completely whole.

"I love you, Gia," he whispered passionately.

"I love you more," she replied, peppering his face with tiny kisses.

This woman, Georgia Ruth Bates, was his beloved. He couldn't wait to show her off to the world as his fiancé and eventually as his wife. This incredible, independent, stubborn, achingly beautiful, and voraciously talented woman named Georgia would forever be on his mind.

THE END

HART & GIA'S PLAYLIST

The story of Hartford Parker and Gia Bates could not have taken place without the influence of music. Here are a few favorites that inspired my writing:

Georgia – Vance Joy
Yours – Russell Dickerson
Perfect – Ed Sheeran
No Ordinary Love – Sade
Can't Stop the Feeling – Justin Timberlake
Written in the Sand – Old Dominion
Tequila – Dan & Shay
Edge of Desire – John Mayer
Ride – Chase Rice
Meant To Be – Bebe Rexhia & FLGA Line
Slow Hands – Niall Horan
The Beautiful Ones – Prince
Georgia On My Mind Ray Charles
Love Is Stronger Than Pride – Sade
Mercy – Brett Young

Enjoy these tunes on the exclusive *Georgia On My Mind* SPOTIFY playlist! https://goo.gl/3mbk6x

FREE SONG DOWNLOAD!
Original Song featured in:

**Georgia Clay
Southern Promises – Book One,
"What Would Happen If…"**

CLICK THE LINK ON MY WEBSITE:
www.kgfletcherauthor.com

ACKNOWLEDGEMENTS

When I wrote Book One (Georgia Clay) in my Southern Promises series, I knew right away that Katie Parker's brother, Hartford, would be the hero in Book Two, (Georgia On My Mind.) I have to give a shout out to my day job peeps in property management who helped me navigate some of the real estate background for Hartford Parker in this book. They really are experts and may have inspired a character or two.

Special thanks to my Almost Elton John leading man, Craig A. Meyer for your feedback regarding all things theater and dance. Our deep dives on tour are my favorite and I love you the most!

Thank you Julie Lamar, a former New York City Rockette, for sharing your audition journey with me. I appreciate the time you took out of your busy life to shed some light on your fascinating career.

To my friend and critique partner, author C.B. Deem, you rock my world! Thank you for kicking my butt during that first love scene that was originally behind closed doors. Glad you liked the re-write! Your unique perspective and feedback is essential to me.

Thank you Eva Talia, my cover artist at Eva Talia Designs – the most patient woman on the planet. When I look at the Southern Promises brand you helped me create, I squeal every time!

To my editor and friend, Vicky Burkholder – thank you for always reigning me in and confidently sharing the finished product with the world. You make me a better writer and a million thanks aren't enough!

For my author friends, ARC & beta readers – you ROCK! I sincerely appreciate the answers to all my endless questions and for sharing my posts. You are an encouraging group and I am honored to support you as well.

For my readers – I honestly love you. Your positive reviews and shares on social media never go unseen. Thank you for taking a chance on me.

To my girlfriends – thanks for putting up with me. I know I disappear when I have deadlines and I'm sorry I miss out on all the fun sometimes. Thank you for your unwavering love and support. You are my Golden Girls.

To my cabana-boy-husband, Ladd - you are my world. Thank you for being my biggest fan. To my gorgeous sons, Hutch, Henry and Hudson – never give up on your dreams! It's never too late to go after them. Mama's proof of that.

Love always wins!
KG
xoxo

ABOUT THE AUTHOR

KG Fletcher is the author of the standalone contemporary romance, *The Nearness of You* and romantic suspense novels, *Love Song* and *Unexpected*. She is currently working on her first series, Southern Promises featuring three standalone romance novels: *Georgia Clay*, *Georgia On My Mind* and *Georgia Pine*. She is an active member of RWA and the Georgia Romance Writers Association. She was a singer/songwriter in Nashville, TN and a recipient of the "Airplay International Award" for "Best New Artist" showcasing original songs at The Bluebird Café. She earned her BFA in theater at Valdosta State College and has traveled the world professionally as a singer/actress. She currently gets to play rock star as a backup singer in the National Tour, "Remember When Rock Was Young – the Elton John Tribute." www.almosteltonjohn.com

KG lives in Atlanta, GA with her husband Ladd and their three gorgeous sons. She is a hopeless romantic continuing her work on her original cabaret act called, *"The Novel Romantic – an unexpected evening of sweet & spicy love"* to help promote her romance novels.

Find KG online:

Website: www.kgfletcherauthor.com

Twitter: www.twitter.com/@kgfletcher3

Instagram: www.instagram.com/kellyf9393/

Facebook: www.facebook.com/kgfletcherauthor/

Amazon: www.Amazon.com/author/kgfletcher

Songs/Cabaret: www.kgfletcherauthor.com/songs--cabaret.html

Pinterest: www.pinterest.com/kfletcher3

Goodreads: www.goodreads.com/book/show/39880601-georgia-on-my-mind

Spotify Playlist: https://goo.gl/3mbk6x

COMING SEPTEMBER/2018
**Book Three in the Southern Promises Trilogy
by KG FLETCHER:**

GEORGIA PINE

The agony of defeat never felt so real.

Never in a million years did Jessica Kaufman think she would be divorced from her real-estate mogul husband and left to raise four young daughters on her own in an affluent Atlanta subdivision. The very last thing she expects is an encounter with her gorgeous gardener who looks more like a sexy beast from her daughters' favorite Disney movie. She is smitten with his evergreen eyes, wild mane of hair and impressive stature.

Tim McGill is in hiding – his reputation and celebrated career on the West Coast left in shambles. He moves far away to distance himself from his downfall and inconspicuously tends the upper-class landscapes to keep his renowned identity a secret. Unlike his typical wealthy clients, Jessica doesn't seem to mind that he's a gardener. One spark between them is all it takes to ignite a fiery passion that could explode if Tim's identity is revealed. He must earn Jessica's trust and finally come to terms with what he has lost.

Can Tim open his heart wide enough to let in a beautiful mother and her four little girls? Or will his Southern Belle turn her back on him and walk away from their happily-ever-after?

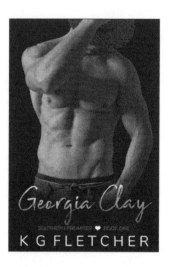

Southern Promises ~ Book One

Everyone in Nashville knows Georgia Clay.

He's the handsome, award-winning songwriter rubbing elbows with the elite stars of country music. An incredible talent in his own right, Clay has always hesitated to step into the spotlight on his own for fear his debilitating childhood secret will rear its ugly head.

Katie Parker is a workaholic Southern beauty who's first love is her career. It's not just her knowledge of the cut-throat insurance business she has skillfully navigated over the years, but her tenacity and gumption in climbing the corporate ladder.

The musician and career woman run into each other in the heat of the Atlanta summer at their ten-year high school reunion and unexpectedly end up in the bed of his pickup truck talking till dawn. As they forge ahead in a passionate long-distance relationship, can Clay admit to Katie she had his heart a long, long time ago? Will her drive and encouragement finally be the reason Georgia Clay takes a chance on his career…and love?

https://www.amazon.com/dp/1732024006/ref=la_B0 1MECVIJ1

More KG Fletcher books!

the nearness of you

KG FLETCHER

Lounge singer, Lauren Rose lived her comfortable life in Atlanta always dreaming of making it in show biz. When she unexpectedly meets British male super-model, David Randle at a gig at the posh St. Regis Hotel, she is swept away by his striking good looks and lilting cadence.

In town for his sister Catherine's nuptials to NASCAR driver, Brian Brady, David invites Lauren to the wedding on a whim. The two instantly bond over music, fashion and family. They continue their new relationship in New York City when David invites Lauren to see him in action at a high-profile fashion shoot for his debut fragrance, "Drive."

Sparks fly when his assistant, Sabrina Watson is none too happy that his new girlfriend has interrupted his grueling, fast-paced schedule. She becomes fixated on separating the happy couple who are falling in love.

Traversing the East Coast and Europe with the paparazzi in hot pursuit, David and Lauren navigate the precarious path of fame, fashion and fate.

https://www.amazon.com/dp/B073MPWGHS

Her heart searched for a melody. Will the love song she finally hears be loud enough to drown out the screaming memories of her past?

Back-up singer Casey lived the old anthem, "work hard, play harder." When she meets handsome sub-drummer, Sam Wildner on a gig, their attraction is immediate. The two musicians forge ahead in a dizzy rhythm of passion and music, both impressed by each other's harmonious abilities. When Sam learns of Casey's family trauma involving her sister's abusive ex-boyfriend, he commits to being there for her and her young niece who is caught in the middle.

The melody of their love song rings loudly in Casey's ears as she and Sam navigate the precarious fast lane of jealousy, murder and rock 'n roll.

https://www.amazon.com/dp/B06XFVWQR2

unexpected

KG FLETCHER

Recently jilted Josephine Davis wasn't looking for love…. A chance encounter along the sweltering highway with Atlanta's own millionaire bachelor changed all that. Devastatingly handsome and full of unexpected talents, William Prescott Harrington, III shows beautiful Josie a life that she could have only dreamed of; his excessive wealth and generosity eventually threatening her very existence. Two star-crossed lovers from polar opposite sides of Atlanta navigate their way through a maze of greed and jealousy desperate for only one thing – each other.

Her heart made a wish. Will her dream become reality or will the nightmare destroy them all?

https://www.amazon.com/dp/B01LYDLUSD

95004508R00157

Made in the USA
Columbia, SC
05 May 2018